CHA

After an attack of pneumonia, Nurse Hilary Hope jumps at the chance of doing some private nursing in France but does not expect her life to be turned upside down by the local devastating doctor there, Raoul de la Rue . . .

CHATEAU NURSE

BY

JAN HAYE

MILLS & BOON LIMITED
London · Sydney · Toronto

First published in Great Britain 1964
as Nurse Hilary's Holiday Task
by Mills & Boon Limited, 15-16 Brook's Mews,
London W1A 1DR

This edition 1981

© Jan Haye 1964

Australian copyright 1981
Philippine copyright 1981

ISBN 0 263 73569 9

Set in 11 on 12 pt Plantin

Made and printed in Great Britain by
Richard Clay (The Chaucer Press) Ltd
Bungay, Suffolk
Photoset by Rowland Phototypesetting Ltd
Bury St Edmunds, Suffolk

CHAPTER ONE

IT was a pleasantly warm day in early August, more typical of spring than high summer, and the two rows of young nurses were glad of this fact, or the occasion might have proved too much for them.

They were the newest graduates of St Oswald's General Hospital, in outer London, to have earned the distinction of becoming State-Registered Nurses, and on a dais erected in the shade of one of the tall elms in the hospital grounds, Sir James Oswestry, the Chairman of the Hospital Board responsible for St Oswald's, was mumbling away at his speech of congratulation and possibly wishing his secretary wasn't a budding journalist at heart.

The nurses, too, who couldn't hear more than an odd word here and there, were wishing the same thing.

'Give us our medals and certificates and let us get off our feet!' was their heartfelt prayer, for some of them had been working all night and should have been tucked up in bed at this hour, while the others had mostly been on duty until dinner-time, after which their various seniors had excused them to change caps, aprons and cuffs and appear spruce and shining on parade.

Matron, with her deputy and the two Sister Tutors, was on the dais enjoying every moment, for she loved speeches about hospital life and duty and rewards well won. The occasion was as important to her as Ascot is to the lover of high fashion, and she had arranged a special tea in her rooms afterwards, for a privileged few. Not the nurses, of course, who had made the occasion possible. As the captain of a ship must lead a lonely life to exact the maximum of discipline from his crew, so Matron kept herself aloof and apart, an authority who could be used as a Court of Appeal only when lower courts had failed to ensure the smooth running of the hospital, or when nurses and Sisters were at loggerheads to such an extent that she was called upon to arbitrate between them.

The speech droned on, and one young nurse glanced at her companion and asked, ventriloquist-wise, without moving her lips.

'I say, Hope, are you all right?'

Hope was the other girl's surname, for nurses usually address one another like boys at school.

'Yes, I'm all right, Davies,' came the reply, 'Why do you ask?'

'You look as white as a sheet.'

'I've been stuck indoors for weeks, you know. But I'm all right, really.'

Hilary Hope was a little touchy on the subject of her health. She had picked up a virus which had laid her low with pneumonia after the strain of final examinations, and though good nursing and a wonderful health had pulled her through, she couldn't understand why she should feel so tired at the moment, as though she would faint if the old boy didn't shut up very soon. If only she could walk about and get her circulation moving she would feel better, but this would only draw attention to her, and she didn't want that. She had travelled up from Sussex this morning to receive her medal and certificate, and also the hospital's gold medal for the best student of her year, and once these honours had been accorded she was to see Matron promptly at five-thirty, after the tea-party, to discuss her return to work, or so she sincerely hoped. A nurse who has been working and studying for almost eighteen hours a day, suddenly finding all the time in the world on her hands, is inclined to be miserable rather than appreciative, and Hilary was no exception.

Once she had become convalescent and was helping her mother in the house, doing the errands and taking Lassie, the labrador, for her walks, village life had suddenly become very dull and limited. A busy hospital is like a small world; in it one can find employment, excitement, friendship, bickering, enjoyment and fulfilment. Hilary could not get back into the swim quickly enough, and as a staff nurse new vistas opened up in unceasing splendour.

Her dark eyes glowed at the prospect and a tiny, dark tendril of hair, escaping from its restraining pins, stirred in the soft, warm breeze as she thought of her future and its possibilities.

'Well, jeep, go on!' Davies' voice cut in on her dreams. '*You're* top of the class and you're to go up now. Are you petrified, or what?'

Automatically Hilary touched her cap and stepped out of line, looking towards the dais where Sister Makepeace, who had instructed the year's best student, was putting a megaphone down by her side and smiling encouragingly.

It seemed a long way to the dais as the waiting nurses clapped their encouragement. Sir James was waiting with hand extended, peering over his pince-nez with smiling, short-sighted pale eyes.

'Well done, my dear. A just and fitting reward. Keep on as you have started and you'll soon be where Matron is today.'

At just twenty-one, Hilary took this to be more a threat than a promise, and murmured her thanks as he handed her the gold medal in its nest of white satin in a red box. She was much more eager to have her State-Registered Nurse's badge, which Sister Wimple, the other tutor, solemnly pinned into place with one single word: 'Congratulations!'

Matron then handed her a certificate tied with red ribbon and the ordeal of walking back to the line was accomplished to further applause.

It was half an hour before all the nurses had received their due honours and were dismissed to take hospital tea before either reporting for duty or going back to bed again until supper time.

Most of the nurses in Hilary's year had already started working as staff nurses, both at St Oswald's and elsewhere.

'I wonder where Watters will send me?' mused Hilary to her friend, Cathy Margrave, who had a prize position as Staff on one of the children's wards.

'I think you'll be going back on your old ward, Hilary. Nobody else has gone to understudy Villiers, and she's getting married and hieing her hence in

October. It's a cinch that you'll step into her shoes because Sister Wedlake spoke so well of you when you were ill.'

'Yes, when I was ill,' grimaced Hilary. 'I suppose she thought I might die and so remembered all my virtues. I don't remember Sister speaking kindly of me when I was working for her.'

'Well, that's the way it goes,' her friend said philosophically, covering a slice of bread liberally with unnaturally red jam. 'They think a little praise mars one's efficiency. But it's you for the female cardiacs. Mark my word.'

'I'd like that,' Hilary decided, lifting the lid of the nearest tea-pot and finding it empty. 'Do you think that would stand more water, Cath? I'm as dry as a desert.'

'Let's make hay,' her friend suggested, and called the dining-room waitress over. 'Do you think the best student of the year deserves a nice fresh brew, Olga? And could you sneak a few cakes from the pantry? Thank *you* my love. You are a darling!'

The waitress went off laughing; the nurses were amusing, and no mistake.

'It's good to be back,' Hilary declared. 'If it wasn't for the food. This stuff they stick on the bread is the kind you can't tell is butter, the variety the T.V. adverts thrive on. My mother can certainly cook.'

'Still,' Cathy said philosophically, as Olga returned with a pot of tea for two and a plate of ginger-bread, which brought the other nurses swarming like flies, 'it's a great life if you don't weaken. I must get back to work now, old thing. It's potty time in my department. Call in and let me known what's happening to you.'

The other nurses began to drift away in ones and twos, and then the dining-room emptied like magic as the Sister in charge of it appeared at the doorway and suggested that the senior staff on duty might be wanting their teas, if it wasn't too much trouble.

Hilary drifted out feeling at a loose end suddenly. It was only half past four and an hour before her appointment with Matron.

'Oh, Nurse Hope!' greeted Sister Dining-room, who boasted that she knew everybody by name; quite an accomplishment when one considered that there were at least three hundred and fifty nursing staff. 'I'm glad you're with us again, but still peaky, eh? You must watch that chest of yours.'

'I'm very well, thank you, Sister. I never have much colour.'

The older woman surveyed her silently. She was a very pretty girl, or one might even say beautiful if it wasn't an extravagant word. Pretty was for blondes with corn-gold hair and bluebell eyes, but this girl was so dark she could have been a daughter of Spain or Islam. Her skin was of that creamy shade which complements dark brown hair and eyes as large and soft as a doe's. But the face was decidedly thinner, the skin stretched over the high cheekbones with a transparency which hadn't previously been obvious.

'It takes time,' Sister Dining-room insisted. 'But why don't you run along and take a look at your old ward while you're waiting? You won't see many old faces among the patients, but Sister and Staff Nurse will be glad to see you.'

It was with a surge of interest that Hilary crossed several hundreds of yards in tiled corridors to Mary Magdalene Ward, where the patients were all women suffering from defective hearts and lungs. The consultant physician in charge of this ward was Sir Hugo Merlin-Smythe, and Hilary faded silently into the sluice as she saw that Sir Hugo, attended by Sister and the staff nurse, were busy behind screens at the far end of the ward.

The junior probationer entered the sluice and said with unfamiliar respect in her tones: 'I say, you won the gold medal, didn't you? I shall never even pass the prelim. The *materia medica* was stinking and I don't think I stand a chance. There's the usual flap on, you know. Mrs Matthews, this time, she has been pretty good for a week or two. But, honestly, I haven't been to tea yet, and I shall drop any minute.'

She departed as hastily as she had arrived, and Hilary wished fervently she had the right to join in the activities of the ward. She was nothing but a fish out of water, and nobody had any time to bother with a mere fish.

She had still only exchanged nods with a harassed Sister Wedlake and heard a muttered 'Congratulations!' from Villiers by the time she was due to see Matron. It wouldn't do to keep the mighty one waiting, so she allowed herself five minutes' grace in the corridor outside the sanctum which was known to the disrespectful as the 'Glory-hole'. This name had evolved from years of disciplinary sessions in which the erring ones, after being soundly ticked-off, were urged to pull up their socks and remember they were members of a team. 'There is glory in being a nurse,' was Matron's final broadside, which gave her office its name.

Promptly on the dot of half past five, Hilary tapped on the door, feeling glad that the moment of decision had arrived.

Matron, who had a door from her private apartments into the office, and tolerated unpunctuality not a jot, was already seated in her swivel chair, her grey hair—the only irresponsible touch about her—dancing in curls around her little lace cap. She wore rimless spectacles which made her eyes look paler than they were, and her dress was brown, relieved by a lace collar and cuffs.

'Nurse Hope,' she said, waving the girl to a chair, an unprecedented gesture, for no nurse ever sat in Matron's presence. 'This must be a wonderful day for you.'

'It is indeed, Matron. I'm so glad to be coming back to work.'

'You got very good marks, you know, Nurse. You may have shattered one or two records. But we all know that it isn't possible to be a good nurse merely on paper, don't we?'

Hilary ventured a smile and waited for more to come.

'I'm very cross with you, Nurse, for insisting on finishing your examinations when you must have been feeling very ill indeed. But as the outcome of all that was so very happy, we'll forget about it, shall we?'

Matron smiled, so Hilary smiled too.

Miss Wattkyn next examined a letter in her hand.

'I have your own doctor's report on your progress here. He says you have made a very good recovery. Our staff physician also gives you a good report. They both suggest you be put on light duties for a while.'

Hilary swallowed. What exactly did 'light duties' mean? 'I would like to get back to work, Matron, *please*,' she said, almost in a tone of desperation.

'Yes, I know you would, Nurse, which is all to your credit, but I really think you should have a holiday first. A busy hospital is no place for invalids, at least not on the staff side. There are no light duties associated with our wards in their present under-staffed state. Half my nurses still have to take their holiday, so that doesn't make the work any lighter. If I put you on a ward, Nurse Hope, you would find yourself doing more than you should. The temptation to go on and do a little more would be too much for you. I simply won't risk it. Another few weeks of taking things easily should do the trick, and I won't spoil a good nurse for the sake of a ha'porth of tar.' Matron had a habit of mixing her metaphors. 'The idea is that you should take a holiday and perhaps do light nursing at the same time. Sir Hugo is still on the premises and he would like to see you. That is all, Staff Nurse.'

Hilary did not notice the significance of her new title in her deep disappointment. She didn't want any more holiday or any wretched light nursing and she felt like telling Sir Hugo so.

She had to pass the children's wards to reach the consultants' sitting-room, and so told her friend the bad news.

'Oh, bad luck,' Cathy said glumly. 'I do miss you, old thing, but your health comes first. You'll probably take some old dowager down to Brighton and help her bathe her corns in the sea, then she'll remember you in her will and you'll never need to work again. One simply must look on the bright side. Well, so long, old thing, we're bathing and bedding at the moment.'

Sir Hugo Merlin-Smythe was a tall, grey-haired ascetic-looking man with patrician features and a voice which became deceptively gentle whenever he was most angry. He was a clever man and could not suffer fools gladly. He had once delivered himself of seven dreadful epithets before the nurse he was addressing realised that she was being 'told off'. The habit had earned him the title of the 'gentle devil', whereas Mr Locket, the senior surgeon, who tore round at great speed, blasting off at everyone, was known as the 'mad devil'.

Sir Hugo heard Hilary's protests in silence and then rang for tea (a consultant could have tea at any hour of the day or night) before clearing his throat.

'I know, my dear, I know,' he sympathised, crossing one long leg over the other and displaying endearing little creased lavender socks round his bony ankles. 'Serious illness is so frustrating when one is active by nature. I had just qualified myself when I had to go into a sanatorium for a full year, and for six

14

months of that time I was on complete rest. It was like a sentence, and I couldn't bear it. But needs must, and I stuck it out and survived. You are so nearly well that it would be foolish to risk losing your whole career for the sake of six more short weeks.'

'L-losing my career, sir?' Hilary echoed.

'Quite easily, m'dear.' The tea arrived, and dainty little sandwiches and cakes such as mere nurses never saw in their dining-room. 'You be mother, and pour. Pneumonia is never a joke, particularly the virus type, and you're lucky to be sitting there at this moment, pouring out the damn' awful tea they dish out here. Nurses have to be tough, and you're toughening up very nicely, but you're not quite there yet. Autumn will come on; mists, chills, overwork, 'flu. As you are now, you'd be a secondary pneumonia like a shot and out of nursing for good. So *we* have to look after you if you won't look after yourself. Understand?'

'Yes, sir, I understand.'

'Well, don't sound so depressed. I've got a nice little job all lined up for you.'

Remembering Cathy's words, Hilary said: 'Such as taking an old dowager to Brighton and bathing her corns in the sea, sir?'

'Yes,' Sir Hugo said brightly. 'Something like that. Only the dowager happens to be an attractive forty-five, and I shouldn't imagine she has corns. She's not active enough for those. Also, substitute for a boarding-house in Brighton a gracious château near Aurillac in the Auvergne district of France, then you'll have hit the nail right on the head.'

15

Hilary opened her mouth like a fish, but said nothing. She was too taken aback.

'You have a passport, I suppose?' Sir Hugo asked.

'Yes, sir. I got it to take a coach tour through Normandy, but I never went. I've never been abroad in my life.'

'Then this is a wonderful opportunity for you to put your schoolgirl French to the test. I'll phone Lady Vesper and ask her to get in touch with you regarding her planned visit to the château. Meanwhile, here is her case history if you would like to read it. You will see that she needs watching more than nursing, but don't allow her to become either angry or excited and she'll jog along very nicely. She has her own doctor out there, of course, but I would always fly out in any emergency. He knows that. Let me have the gen back when you've finished with it.'

Hilary took this as a dismissal and went along to the outpatients' hall to read the notes in her possession. Outpatients was deserted at this hour, though the nearby casualty department was in its usual ferment.

Lady Vesper had a congenitally weak heart. She had almost died during her two confinements and had been forbidden to have any more children. She was subject to fainting attacks when over-tired and had gone into heart failure during a recent attack of jaundice. With such a case it always meant taking precautions to avoid overstrain rather than treating any definite disease. Illness was bad for the patient in that the naturally recuperative functions of the body put an extra demand upon the weak heart. On the other hand, for long periods the patient could live a normal and happy existence; there was no pain, and it was a case of cutting one's cloth according to one's needs, physically speaking.

Hilary spent the night at the hospital and returned to her home the next day full of news of her unexpected luck.

'It's like being paid to have a holiday,' she told her mother. 'I shall have practically nothing to do but laze around and get fat.'

'Which you can do with,' said Mrs Hope, looking at her daughter's slimness somewhat critically. 'Don't you ever think of getting married, dear?' she asked suddenly and surprisingly.

'Whom, for instance?'

'Well, Ted's a very nice boy . . . '

'Ted!' Hilary's voice consigned Ted Willis, who was the son of a local farmer, to the realms of the ridiculous. 'Honestly, Mother, because *you* were married at eighteen you try to make me feel I'm on the shelf. I would like to get married, some day, but there's my career to think of. I haven't studied and worked these three years to get married just when the whole nursing world is my oyster. Look at this trip to France, for instance. It's only because I'm now a qualified nurse that I'm being given the opportunity.'

'You live your own life, of course,' Mrs Hope said, with a shrug, implying that no career was as good for a woman as the domestic one nature intended.

Hilary's two sisters, Helen and Jean, were both married and had children; seeing them so happy, with good, steady husbands, Mrs Hope couldn't help feeling concerned about her youngest chick and her future happiness.

Hilary was also concerned for her future happiness, however, and often gave the opposite sex a good deal of thought, wondering if one of them would one day contribute towards that happiness. She wasn't in love with any of the doctors or students at the hospital, as many of her fellows were, and none of the boys in her home village interested her more than as friends and occasional companions. She sometimes wondered if she was abnormal in this respect; perhaps she was under-sexed. But there were times when she knew she hadn't met the right man to stir her to raptures. Sometimes she walked in the quiet lanes and woods near her home, and occasionally would come upon a familiar view made beautiful by a seasonal carpet of bluebells or gilded with tints of autumn. At such times she played a little game and turning to an unseen companion would remark: 'Darling, isn't that breathtaking!'

Who 'darling' was, she never quite knew, but he was real to her in everything but the flesh, and she would unconsciously be looking for him until she found him, and—her mother would have been gratified to know—she hoped it wouldn't be too long before he appeared, career or not.

Thoughts of a romantic nature were hustled aside when the telephone rang with a message from Lady Vesper, who was to be her holiday patient. Her ladyship was recovering from one of her attacks at an expensive nursing home in Surrey, and she expressed a wish that Nurse Hope would call and have tea with her the following day to discuss their plans.

The next afternoon Hilary dressed carefully but quietly, as befitted a trained nurse wearing mufti, in a plain tan suit and a blouse of a daffodil shade. Her hair, dark and plentiful, she wore in a bun, and pulling on new tan gloves, which matched her handbag, she set off on the train for Guildford and then took a bus out to 'Redroofs'.

As she rang the front door bell a young man came hurriedly out of the house and almost knocked her flying. Her handbag did go hurtling, shedding its contents all over the gravelled drive.

'I say, I'm most awfully sorry!' said the offender, stooping and picking up a lipstick, a diary, a library ticket and a book of stamps in one large hand. 'Please do call me a few suitably horrible names, and then I might feel better!'

Looking at him with a smile—he was about her own age and had fair, unruly hair and clear blue eyes—she didn't want to call him horrible names at all.

'That's all right,' she assured him. 'It was an accident.'

'If you're sure you're all right, not winded or anything, I'll dash. I have a train to catch.'

'Then please do. There's nothing wrong with me.'

'It was a pleasure bumping into you,' he smiled with easy charm, and began to travel in long easy strides down the wide drive.

When Hilary saw Lady Vesper she realised that she had just met her son. The likeness was unmistakable, although her ladyship's fair hair was now kept bright by unnatural means and her blue eyes were a little faded by illness.

'My dear, let me look at you,' she said. 'You're rather young, aren't you?'

'I'm twenty-one, Lady Vesper,' Hilary said promptly. 'And I'm now State Registered. Also, I spent six months on the cardiac ward in my hospital.'

'Yes, I'm sure you're all that Hugo makes you out to be,' Lady Vesper said somewhat impatiently. 'But young people are inclined to crave gaiety and excitement. There isn't much of either at the Château des Bois.'

'I don't expect gaiety and excitement when I'm working,' Hilary said promptly. 'Frankly I shall be glad to have something to do.'

'Ah, yes,' Lady Vesper nodded her head. 'I believe *you* have been ill, too?'

'I'm over it now,' Hilary said confidently. 'But Sir Hugo says I musn't go back to the hospital for at least six weeks.'

Lady Vesper rang for tea, and during the light meal which was served to them she gently drew what information she could from her visitor, not only about her home and family but about boy friends, too.

'I haven't any,' Hilary told her frankly. 'At least, nothing serious. I have been too busy with exams and one thing and another to bother with men.'

She was a very pretty girl, though, Lady Vesper decided rather craftily. It might not come amiss to have such a prize actually living in the château.

'I have a son, you know,' she volunteered, as her thoughts took shape. 'He may well decide to come out and visit us.'

'That will be nice for you,' Hilary answered, but a peculiar thrill went through her when she remembered that large, rather disconcerting young man bundling all her things back into her bag.

'It will be nice for you, too. He must take you about and show you the country.'

'This is too much!' Hilary thought faintly. 'To have both a holiday *and* a handsome escort! I'm beginning to think I'll wake up in a minute.'

'My daughter is at finishing school in Paris, but at the moment she and a friend are holidaying at St Tropez. No doubt when pleasure palls we shall also see Louisa. Since I gave up our London house, which was really too much for me, London is so exhausting, the château is the only family home we possess. I practically live here, of course, when I'm in England, and apart from the nursing angle one can usually rake up a four for bridge, which helps the time along. But I'm longing to get back to St Jude and the Bois. England in August can be extremely enervating. So will it be convenient for you if we fly out next Wednesday?'

'Er—er—certainly, my lady.'

'Then you had better come here on Tuesday and help me to pack. They'll give you a bed for the night, I'm sure, and you'll be on hand to drive with me to the airport next morning. It's warm in Auvergne during the day, but cool at night, so go prepared for the climate. Of course you will be wearing uniform except when you're off duty. You understand that?'

'Certainly, my lady.'

'Then I think that will be all for now. I'm tired.'

'Can I do anything for you? Get you anything?'

'There are people here to do that,' Lady Vesper said rather shortly, and feeling herself to be dismissed, Hilary said good afternoon and left the nursing home, her mind suddenly in a whirl of anticipation and excitement.

CHAPTER TWO

THE journey to southern France was a series of vivid impressions to Hilary, most of them pleasant. She had never flown before, for one thing, and almost fainted with sheer excitement the moment before take-off.

'You're looking pale,' Lady Vesper remarked, as her young companion fumbled with her seat-belt. 'I hope you're not air-sick, or anything like that?'

'I'm sure not,' Hilary said firmly. 'I'm just naturally pale.'

'It would be too ridiculous if I was landed with looking after you.'

Hilary merely smiled. She had a feeling that Lady Vesper was not entirely in love with her young nurse and that she would have to prove herself before she was accepted.

The aircraft suddenly felt weightless as it rose into the air and Hilary held on to her stomach—which had also apparently tried to take flight—and was relieved to find that she was feeling merely exhilarated and very happy. It was mid-morning and strange to be on top of the white, downy clouds rather than under them. Up here the sun shone constantly, and, occasionally, between the clouds, one caught a glimpse of Liliputian towns and villages and what remained of England before the dark swell of the Channel was a variegated green map.

'Lady Vesper—?' Hilary queried as her companion sat with heavily veined lids shut and slightly creased.

'Be quiet, girl! I was up early and I'm trying to sleep.'

'Sorry, my lady.'

Hilary admitted to herself that the only fly in the ointment was going to be her patient. She was intolerant and unkind. Often people with her complaint were selfish and self-centred, but one had to understand and be patient with them. It would never do to snap back and upset them. In a way they were mildly tyrannical.

She looked at the woman and decided that she had once been very pretty. Her face was oval and the mouth, though now somewhat petulant, was full and well shaped. She had small ears and wore pink pearl studs. These showed up the blue tinge of her skin, and when the stewardess appeared with refreshments, Hilary touched her companion firmly.

'Lady Vesper, you must have a warm drink. You can go to sleep again afterwards.' She gazed firmly into the irritable blue eyes. 'Milk or meat extract?' she asked, without once wavering.

The other sat upright with a sigh.

'I can see Hugo has been at you. I thought you were too young to be bossy, but you're not. Meat extract, please. Little and often is how I like my nourishment.'

Hilary mentally chalked herself a score up on an invisible board and decided that to be tough with

Lady Vesper, when the occasion demanded, was to earn her grudging respect. In other words, she was herself a 'boss' and so appreciated being 'bossed'.

They were now skimming over a France divided into neat little green squares. Dark green lines indicated poplar-edged roads, and they all appeared to lead to Paris where the aircraft landed at Orly airport. Here Hilary and her companion changed to a lighter plane which took off, after an irritating delay, for Lyons. Most of the other passengers and the stewardess were French, and Hilary practised her '*nons*' and '*ouis*' with a conviction that her schoolgirl vocabulary was going to be greatly increased before she once again returned to her native shore.

At Lyons, after the formalities of Customs and Immigration, they were met by a large, comfortable Simca limousine, chauffeur-driven. The French chauffeur, Gaston, was very happy to see his mistress. They spoke in rapid French for ten minutes or more, and Hilary realised that knowing all about the whereabouts of the pen of one's father's aunt wasn't going to be much use here. She had a French-English phrase book among her possessions, however, and determined to learn a little more of the language every day.

Lady Vesper was uncommunicative during the long drive, and Hilary did not pester her with questions. She saw by the signposts that they circled the town of Vichy, famous for its tonic water and as the seat of a capitulated France's government during the last war. Always now was the threat of the mountains looming ahead, and as they drove through a town in a

25

lush valley, Clermont Ferrand, it was called, the Simca headed straight for the mountains and, magically, they opened up and there was a good metalled road climbing up and up, at first gently and then sharply into horseshoe bends looming over distant valleys which looked like pie-plates with circling vineyards hemming them in, and from which the motorist was separated only by his own prayers and a low stone parapet, not more than a foot high, at the business side of the road.

The air was now like wine, thin and rarefied. Lady Vesper shivered and Hilary tucked a thick rug cosily about her.

Through the high *massif*, Gaston drove the car smoothly and expertly. Lady Vesper dozed, but Hilary, although she was now very tired, couldn't bear to miss a moment of the experience. She looked at her charge and hoped that she would never become so used to wonderful things that she didn't even notice them. The mountain descent was almost as hair-raising as the ascent had been, although now she was assured that Gaston knew what he was about and didn't feel like shrieking every time she looked over the parapet into what could so easily be eternity. The town of Aurillac was pleasantly situated in a valley with the *massif* at its door, and half an hour later, after driving through scenery which was suggestive at times of the Yorkshire dales and at others of Torquay, with squat, feather-duster palms bobbing up in unexpected places and reminding one that the Mediterranean was really not so very far away, the car climbed a gentle hill, entered a well-wooded area at about five hundred feet of mixed birch and oak trees, climbed again, through pines, and arrived in the village of St Jude, thirty or fewer little white-washed houses clustering round a red-roofed church. Just outsde the village the Château des Bois sat on a ledge cut into the hill and looked blandly forth over its acres. It was the most beautiful house Hilary had ever seen, and she gasped in admiration as she saw the two flights of Italian marble steps leading up to a wide terrace over which bougainvillea rioted in an orderly, colourful manner. The front of the house was flat, almost Georgian-looking, but there was an elegance about doorway and window which was entirely French, and one would not have been surprised to see the original Cinderella come running, slipper-less, down those marble steps away from the gaiety and glory of the ball taking place within.

Lady Vesper was watching her companion narrowly.

'You like my house, Nurse Hope?'

'Oh, my lady, it's a beautiful house! I—I haven't words.'

'Then you think I did rightly, when I had to choose, to keep this place on?'

Hilary looked at her, her young face lit up like a lamp. 'You must be very proud of the château, Lady Vesper, and I'm proud to be invited here.'

'You're quite a nice child. I wish Louisa were more like you. She thinks of the Bois as a mausoleum. I shall go straight to my room and rest and I shan't get up at all tomorrow. You may come and see me about nine-thirty to give me my tablets, but don't hang

27

about, apart from that, looking officious. I have a maid, Marie, who has looked after me for years, and we mustn't offend her, but she'll ring for you if I need you. Try and occupy yourself as best you can. The housekeeper will show you your room.'

Gaston swept up his mistress as though she had been a child and carried her up the steps, and Hilary followed, feeling rather helpless and carrying her hand luggage. The procession passed through the main doors into a wide, marble-floored hall where the staff was assembled. There was the housekeeper, Gaston's wife, wearing a jingling chatelaine round her waist, the elderly maid, Marie, already embracing her mistress with her face blotched with tears and two maids, and a *garçon*, who looked slightly idiotic and had his two younger colleagues constantly in fits of giggles.

The youngsters fled back to the kitchen as soon as they were able, and Gaston carried Lady Vesper up the broad central staircase with his wife and Marie in close attendance. Hilary was left standing in the hall, suddenly feeling a long way from home and rather miserable after the hectic excitement of the day.

So this is what it felt like to be a 'foreigner', having a language tossed all around you which you didn't understand and then being ignored, like a piece of wood.

The hall was beautiful, with Watteau shepherds and shepherdesses muralled on the walls and ceiling in Arcadian settings of eternal summer, but Hilary didn't want to stand examining them all evening. It was now almost seven o'clock and she had been awakened from her little hard bed at the nursing home at half past four that morning.

Eventually the jingling of keys announced the housekeeper's return. She came downstairs muttering apologetically, which Hilary assumed to mean: 'I'm sorry, but in all the excitement I had forgotten you.'

Then her black, boot-button eyes shot a dart of enquiry.'

'*Parlez français?*'

'*Un peu,*' Hilary said awkwardly.

Madame then proceeded to speak slowly in her provincial French, which Hilary failed to understand. She understood the beckoning finger, however, and followed Madame up the stairs, along a wide carpeted corridor to a room at the far end. It was not a very large room, but Hilary was delighted with it, for it had one window which overlooked the terrace and, in consequence, the valley below, and another which stared into the blackness of a pinewood to the right of the house. Each window opened on to a small balcony and the air was sweet with the scent of the pines and rapidly cooling after the heat of the day.

One of the maids brought her a meal on a tray before going home to the village for the night. She stared at the English girl coolly and with a certain amount of hostility. She did not attempt conversation and waited scarcely long enough to hear Hilary's *merci* as the tray was set down on a table near the south window.

There was a cup of clear soup, a veal cutlet and a

bowl of salad, rolls, butter and cheese and a dish of grapes. The housekeeper herself brought a jug of coffee and removed the tray, gratified that her young guest apparently enjoyed a healthy appetite. As she said goodnight on her way out, it appeared that nobody was expecting the young nurse to do much that evening but have a bath and retire to her bed. Hilary was so tired that she found herself nodding off in the bath. As she had brought her own travelling clock with her, she set the alarm for nine-fifteen and crept into bed to sleep for two hours until it should be time to give Lady Vesper her sleeping pills. She was surprised to find that sleep did not come immediately, however. She had been too excited all day, and now the chain of events passed behind her closed eyes like a kaleidoscope. Sometimes there was a snake-like road unwinding like a ribbon, and at others people she had passed, standing in cottage doorways or at street corners, appeared so vividly she could even recognise their features.

No sooner had she slipped into an uneasy doze than the alarm rang, and she started up in confusion, wondering where she was and why.

It was dark now, and the mountain air blew chill through the wide-open windows. She was glad she had brought her warm dressing-gown instead of buying a new silk one, and wrapping herself up in this she went out in search of her patient's room.

The next morning coffee, rolls and delicious *croissants* were served to Hilary in her room at a little after eight.

She felt wonderfully refreshed and eager for

activity, so took a bath and then went along to see how Lady Vesper had slept.

Her ladyship said not at all, but her eyes were quite clear and she was obviously enjoying her breakfast.

'You're staying in bed today, my lady?' Hilary inquired.

'Yes, or at least, in my room. As you can see, I am very comfortable here.'

'When would you like to take a bath?'

'What is that to you? I'm perfectly capable of bathing myself.'

Hilary flushed and then took a firm stand once again.

'Sir Hugo has instructed me always to stand by while you're in the bath, my lady. I wouldn't be doing my duty if I disobeyed these instructions.'

Lady Vesper tried to stare the young nurse out and then, failing, said something to her maid in French. Marie laughed rather maliciously and glanced at Hilary, who didn't flinch. It wouldn't be for long that they could make remarks she didn't understand, she was determined on that score.

'What time will you bath, Lady Vesper?' she asked patiently.

'Oh, in half an hour, girl!' the other snapped, and Hilary quietly left the room with the conviction that Lady Vesper was quite happy among her familiars at the château, people who had known and served her for many years. It must have been Sir Hugo who had insisted upon her taking a nurse with her on this occasion, and so far the nurse was being made to appear both a nuisance and a fool.

31

But Hilary was as determined to do her duty as her patient was to resist her, and promptly at half past nine she went along to her ladyship's suite and ran the bath without more ado. She did not intrude while the woman took her bath, though she left the door ajar and her ear was attuned to all movement within. It was Marie who was summoned, however, to dress her ladyship in a fresh nightdress and a flowing negligée.

When they both emerged, chattering like two sparrows, Hilary was waiting with the injection which her patient was to have twice a day.

'Oh, what a bore!' Lady Vesper submitted unwillingly and then curled up once more in bed. 'Now that I've been duly supervised in my ablutions and medicated, perhaps I can have a little peace, Nurse?'

'Certainly, my lady. Your next injection is due at six-thirty. Perhaps you will let me know if you require me in the meantime?'

Lady Vesper was eyeing her steadily.

'You know, my girl, you have the nicest way of being insolent of anybody I know. You're too intelligent not to realise that your patience and tolerance are anathema to someone like me.'

Hilary gave a slight shrug of helplessness.

'I don't intend to be insolent, Lady Vesper, but I don't quite know how to handle you.'

'Handle me? Is that what you're supposed to do?'

'I have to perform certain services which you apparently resent. If I kept out of your way altogether, which you obviously would prefer, I would be failing in my duty as your nurse. You need my services

32

because of your health, and it's up to me to find a way of helping you without irritating you. That's what I mean by not knowing how to handle you. But I'll learn.'

There was another meeting of the eyes, and this time there were small sparks flashing from Hilary's.

'I made you angry, didn't I?'

'Not really. A good nurse doesn't get angry.'

'Well, let's say you're not quite good enough yet.'

A sudden smile illuminated Lady Vesper's countenance and she looked ten years younger when she smiled. 'I shall take an interest in your handling of me from now on. What does your father do?'

'He was a solicitor, but he died last year.'

'Oh, I'm sorry. Well, run off and occupy yourself now. You'll find plenty to do, no doubt, and I shall be perfectly all right. Dr de la Rue is coming to see me this afternoon about four, so you'd better show up to meet him. He'll probably tell you how difficult he finds me to handle, too, so you'll have something in common.'

Hilary left the room feeling that Lady Vesper liked her a little better for their exchange. She was amused in an odd way and had made play of the word 'handle' as though she liked to be regarded as a difficult customer.

The girl changed out of uniform into a dark pink shift dress with a pointed collar. She consulted her phrase-book and told the housekeeper, Madame Durand, that she would not be in to lunch. She also informed her that she could be found in the village, and sallied forth, feeling suddenly happy and adventurous.

She wanted to find someone who could instruct her in French; now she regretted not having persisted with the language after leaving school, and decided that where there was a village there would be a school, and a schoolmaster, or so she hoped.

She had forgotten that during August all schools have a habit of closing, however, but she did find the schoolmaster's mother who, understanding the problem after a conversation in pidgin French on the one hand and pidgin English on the other, recommended that Mademoiselle should seek our Monsieur Smees, the English painter, who taught his own language to French people as a sideline, so why not the reverse? Madame added further that Monsieur would no doubt be at the café at this hour.

Hilary thanked the kindly woman and wandered down the narrow cobbled street, feeling the sun warm on her shoulders. A cluster of colourful umbrellas, like gay mushrooms, told the whereabouts of the small café, and here she saw a number of elderly local men, wearing blue cotton shirts and berets, and a young man with sandy hair and that white skin which freckles in strong light, looking so English he stood out like a sore thumb in that company. He had a glass of coffee near his elbow and was busy with a charcoal pencil and a sketching pad getting quite a good likeness of a hawk-nosed old man drinking brandy and soda nearby.

'Monsieur Smees?' Hilary queried, somewhat shyly.

The very blue eyes of the redhead regarded her.

'*Oui*?'

'Er—my name is Hilary Hope. I'm staying at the château.'

'Oh, you're English. Actually the name's Smith.'

Hilary laughed, and Michael Smith surveyed her appreciatively.

'I agree that "Smees" *is* a little more distinguished,' he smiled. 'What can I do for you?'

Over coffee Hilary told him about herself and her difficulty in communicating with the staff at the château.

'Yes, British schools don't exactly equip one for travelling,' he agreed. 'But it soon comes when one has to sink or swim. How can I help?'

'I thought you might agree to give me lessons.'

'Well, that would be a new angle. But I don't profess to be a French scholar. I merely get along.'

'That's what I want to do.'

'O.K., then. How about right now and every morning at eleven?'

Hilary found herself remembering a lot she thought she had forgotten when, for the next half hour, Michael Smith spoke to her in nothing but French, with a greal deal of mime. She even found herself wishing him *au revoir* as they parted, quite naturally.

She had bought some rolls and sausage from the café together with a bottle of mineral water, and Michael had told her of an excellent picnic spot high up in the pinewoods. The midday heat was now quite excessive for someone newly out from England, and she was glad to plunge into the shade of the trees as she found a path deep in pine needles. Occasionally she caught a glimpse of the château; it was so imposing that it was difficult not to see for many miles around.

Hilary walked and climbed until she was tired and then found a shady dell in which to enjoy her picnic. Not a soul was about. After the meal it seemed natural to close one's eyes and enter a state of limbo which was not quite sleep but rather a stupor induced by the afternoon heat and the disinfectant scent of the pines. She roused herself with a start to see, by her watch, that it was three o'clock. She was supposed to report to Lady Vesper's doctor at four, and so had better make a beeline for the château rather than return to the village.

The pinewood opened out into a chain of fields, which she was sure belonged to the château, and so she climbed a fence and stepped boldly through a herd of fine Charollais cattle. She was negotiating the third of such fields when a voice brought her up sharply in her tracks.

'*Arretez! Vous ne seriez pas être ici.*'

The voice was masculine, sharp and obviously annoyed. Hilary saw a tall, dark-haired man approaching her with a scowl upon his patrician features.

'*Pardon!*' she said in a small voice.

He pointed towards the fence where there were holds for climbing over. '*Allez-vous en, s'il vous plaît.*'

She went, feeling humiliated and angry, only sorry that her French was too limited for her to answer back and inform the farmer, or bailiff, whoever he was, that there were nice ways of asking people to go away and that it wouldn't do him any harm to learn a few of them.

Carefully avoiding other fields she found her way back to the château, arriving at a quarter to four, which just gave her time to freshen up and change her dress. She wore a sleeveless white one this time, with pink dots all over it. Already the sun had caught her face and arms and flushed her skin under its natural olive tint.

She knocked at Lady Vesper's room door as the ormolu clock on the landing struck four. Marie opened the door and indicated that her ladyship was already in conversation with someone. Looking past her, Hilary saw her patient draped on a chaise-longue near the wide-open windows; a striped sun-blind kept the sun's rays from entering and diffused a rosy light which was extremely flattering to Lady Vesper. The broad-shouldered figure of a man occupied a chair near the chaise-longue and looked vaguely familiar, though Hilary knew this to be absurd as she hadn't had time to know anyone in St Jude apart from Michael Smith.

'Well, come in if you're coming in, Nurse Hope!' Lady Vesper called out somewhat irritably. 'Come over her and meet *Monsieur le docteur*. He has just been scolding me for daring to suggest that I entertain a few friends to dinner now and again. Nurse Hope —Dr de la Rue.'

'Good afternoon, Doctor,' Hilary said, standing automatically to attention.

'Nurse and I have already met, in a roundabout way,' Dr de la Rue smiled, and his patrician face became transformed by amusement.

'You!' Hilary exclaimed, flushing hotly at the remembrance and seething all over again.

'Yes,' the doctor addressed Lady Vesper, whose raised brows were querying this exchange, 'I saved Nurse from being tossed by my large, very fierce Charollais bull, Napoleon the Fifth. She was idling across the field where I allow him free range for grazing. Of course now that I know Nurse is English, I understand. Nobody from the village would be so foolish as to tempt providence like that.'

The English was perfect with faintly French inflections here and there. It was a charming voice with a delightful accent, but Hilary hated it because it was now laughing at her.

'I saw no bull,' she said sharply. 'And *you* were walking in the field.'

'Like all good bulls Napoleon knows his master. But nice little girls in pink dresses are inclined to bring out his bullying instincts. Ah!' He was entirely French now as he threw up his hands. 'I make a pun!'

Hilary's countenance retained a stony stare, however, and he shrugged as he returned his attention to the patient.

'Now, my dear, I think we'll listen in to this chest of yours. Nurse!'

Hilary undid the ribbons of the negligée and stood by while the stethoscope travelled over the pale surface of the invalid's bosom. She stole a glance at the doctor's face, engrossed by what his ears told him, and admitted that he was very good-looking in an aristocratic way. His hair was plentiful and black, but his eyes were a clear, pale grey. He could be anything from thirty to thirty-five.

'Right!' he said, meeting Hilary's gaze with another smile of amusement. 'Shall we go where this naughty person can't hear us?'

'No more restrictions, now, Raoul,' Lady Vesper called after him as he shepherded the girl towards the door. 'I've had enough of those. When you've finished come and join me for tea. You can get some downstairs, Nurse Hope.'

'So that's put me in my place,' Hilary pondered wryly as Dr de la Rue shut the door and then paced the corridor outside as though wondering what to say. 'I'm not invited to the tea-party.'

'She must be very careful,' Dr de la Rue at last said seriously. 'There is simply no power there. None at all.'

'She doesn't take too kindly to my telling her what and what not to do, sir,' Hilary informed him.

'But then,' he shrugged again, 'we none of us take kindly to other people's advice, do we? You, Nurse, resent being told to go away from angry bulls, and our dear Caroline resents being told she has not the strength to lead the normal life she craves. What to do? We must be tactful but very firm. You sleep in the dressing-room?'

'No. I'm at the far end of the corridor.'

'Then that must be changed. You should be near her in the night.'

'Marie, the maid, musn't be upset, or so Lady Vesper says.'

'Leave Marie to me, and Lady Vesper also. I see no

reason to increase the drugs she is taking already, providing she leads a very quiet life, but in emergency I'll leave you three ampoules. Inject thirty-five C.C.S. and then send for me. Only in emergency. You do understand?'

'I understand, Doctor.'

Hilary took the ampoules and with a brief salute of a long, slim hand he left her and returned to his patient.

About an hour later the *garçon* arrived at Hilary's room and indicated that she must collect her things together immediately. He carried her cases along the corridor into a small room adjoining her ladyship's suite, to which there was a communicating door. There was no balcony and only one window, but the girl did not regret the change, for she felt more responsible towards her patient now that she was on hand.

Once again she unpacked and had just finished when she was summoned into the presence by Marie.

'Nurse Hope,' Lady Vesper inquired, 'why were you not in uniform when Dr de la Rue called?' The girl was silent. She hadn't expected to be taken to task on this account. 'Are you my nurse or a house guest here? I thought I told you to wear uniform at all times except when you were off duty.'

'I'm sorry, my lady,' Hilary murmured, humiliated for a second time that day. 'I didn't think.'

'Well, you must think. I expect a nurse to look like a nurse if I'm to have one. I don't ask much of your time, but when I need you I don't want you coming in here in tennis clothes or looking as though you're about to attend a garden party. That will be all.'

Hilary changed into uniform immediately, wondering if the holiday task to which she had looked forward so much was going to be so wonderful after all. In hospital one knew exactly what was expected of one, when to wear uniform and when to wear mufti. Here at the château, in its unique and beautiful setting, Lady Vesper was a decided fly in the ointment. She pounced without warning, putting one firmly in one's place; at one moment telling one to keep out of the way and the next grousing because one wasn't in the full uniform of the nursing profession. The idea of putting on a starched dress and apron and making up a cap for the sake of watching a doctor using his stethoscope was slightly ridiculous, but when one couldn't tell a patient she was being ridiculous, because of the risk of upsetting her, it was even more tiresome.

'If I'm her nurse, and *not* a house guest, I'll jolly well do my job thoroughly,' Hilary decided. 'All day I've felt slightly like a fish out of water. The holiday part is all right providing I'm allowed to do the task part as well.'

With a gleam in her eye, Hilary sailed into her ladyship's room, after she had had her evening meal, with a covered tray in her hands.

'What are you doing, Nurse?' Lady Vesper asked. She was playing patience at a table near the window, which was now closed against the cooling, evening air.

'I've come to give you a talcum rub, my lady. You'll find it most refreshing and it will help your circulation. Will you come on the bed, please?'

'Don't be ridiculous. I'm in the middle of a game.'

'Then I'll wait.'

Hilary stood hovering, like Nemesis, until Lady Vesper became nervous and irritated.

'Dear me! You *are* a tiresome girl. I'm sure I would have got it out if you hadn't put me off. All right.' She sighed crossly. 'What do you want me to do?'

Hilary was certain that her patient enjoyed the brisk, fragrant massage, though she never admitted it. After it was over she yawned and said: 'I believe you know that if I once got into bed I wouldn't get out again tonight. Well, you've won. I'll have my injections and tablets, and disturb me again if you dare!'

Hilary smiled as she prepared the injection.

'I think tomorrow you should go out for a drive, Lady Vesper. It would do you good.'

'I'll decide what does me good, young woman. I've had plenty of experience, more than you.'

'Your appetite is poor. A little of the mountain air would sharpen it.'

'You don't give up, do you, Nurse?' the other said with grudging admiration. 'Like water wearing at a stone you get your way.'

'I shall only insist on things for your own good, my lady. You can depend on that.'

Hilary had administered the injection and was getting a drink for the woman to take her sleeping tablets, when there was an interruption. Marie entered the room and jabbered in French in some agitation.

Lady Vesper waved away the sleeping tablets with

an imperious hand.

'Later, Nurse.' She had flushed and looked very pretty, though anger rather than pleasure had obviously brought this on. She spoke sharply to Marie, then turned on the young nurse.

'I'm not as tired as I thought. There is a visitor coming to see me.' As Hilary looked dubious she proceeded: '*Not* an assignment with a gentleman, Nurse, but a young girl, about your age. She lives locally.' She suddenly regarded Hilary as though for the first time. It was the same calculating look she had given her at their first meeting, before telling her she had a son.

'How would you like to run along, Nurse, and put on that pretty white dress you had on when Raoul was here?' Hilary looked incredulous. 'It made you look so very attractive. I like to see girls looking fresh and sweet.'

'But why must I change now? What's happening?'

'I want you to meet this girl, Celeste Beldame. Come back when you've changed.'

Hilary didn't argue any further, for at times Lady Vesper's mind and its workings were beyond her. Why she couldn't have met Mademoiselle Beldame while wearing uniform, she couldn't imagine, and it was Lady Vesper herself who had complained about her wearing mufti in the sickroom only a few hours previously.

Nevertheless she donned the white dress with its tiny pink dots and did her hair in a less severe style, so that it was loosely knotted in her nape and shone with brushing.

When she reappeared in Lady Vesper's room there was an animated conversation in progress, and she would rather not have interrupted it.

'Ah!' Lady Vesper greeted her gladly. 'This is Hilary now.' She made the introductions before Hilary had got over the shock of being addressed by her Christian name. Apparently the girl, Celeste, spoke about as much English as Hilary did French. After a stumbled ''Ow do you do,' she was silent, and they regarded one another surreptitiously from time to time while the older woman did all the talking.

Celeste was a striking-looking redhead, with hair of a titian shade and eyes as green as those of a cat. She did not look at all happy now that Hilary was present in the room.

'Isn't Celeste kind?' Lady Vesper turned to her nurse to inquire. 'She's going to accompany me on that drive you suggested I take tomorrow. We shall have a picnic up in the hills.'

'Very nice,' Hilary smiled, wondering if she, too, would be invited.

'You can keep an eye on things here, my dear,' milady answered her silent hopes. 'Celeste and I have much to talk about.'

In French she then turned to the other girl and told her she was tired and must settle down for the night. She would see her, she added, the next morning at eleven.

'Très bien, madame. Bon soir!'

'Bon soir, Celeste.'

'Bon soir, Mademoiselle 'Ope!'

'Bon soir.'

44

Celeste favoured Hilary with a final narrow-eyed glance before she departed. There was an air of intrigue in the room which Hilary didn't quite understand.

'She's the daughter of the local vet, you know,' her ladyship volunteered. 'A little nobody, really.'

So Lady Vesper was a snob, Hilary decided. But why take the girl off on a picnic if she despised her? How did Celeste come to be visiting the château in the first place? Apart from a large fat tabby cat there were no animals on the estate whatsoever.

'Have you had dinner yet, Nurse?' her ladyship asked, all the warmth of sudden friendship now disappeared from her voice.

'No, not yet, my lady.'

'Then go and get it. You should know your way around by now. The dining-room is off the hall. It was opened up today on my instructions because my son, Verian, is expected tomorrow. He is motoring down from Dieppe. He may arrive while I am out, so do make him welcome. You need not wear uniform tomorrow. That will be all, Nurse.'

Hilary went off in search of the dining-room, feeling cheered by the news that she was to meet Verian Vesper once more. He had appeared to be an attractive young man, and with him about the place the château would not seem so vast and so lonely. She pondered Lady Vesper's invitation for her to wear mufti as an invitation to make herself attractive for Verian's benefit, and though the suggestion surprised her she was not going to argue about it.

Though she and Lady Vesper's heir had merely

'bumped into one another,' quite literally, the impact had been a lingering one with her. In fact, now that all those examinations were truly a thing of the past, she could afford to be feminine and welcome a little masculine attention.

The cooking at the château left quite a lot to be desired, but as she finished her lonely meal with plenty of black coffee and cream and a dish of the local grapes, she smiled contentedly and settled down to write home with the conviction that the morrow would prove to be an interesting day at the very least.

CHAPTER THREE

HILARY awoke in the small divan bed which had been set up in the dressing-room for her use, with the conviction that something wonderful illuminated the day. When she remembered who was expected, she told herself severely that she had no right to entertain any hopeful thoughts about Lady Vesper's only son, but her anticipatory pleasure remained undiminished as she enjoyed her breakfast—apparently breakfast in bed was the tradition at the Château des Bois—and then went to her patient's room to supervise her bathing and a talcum rub, which her ladyship now asked for and apparently enjoyed.

Marie then took over, somewhat jealously, and helped her mistress to dress.

Down in the kitchens the picnic was being prepared, slices of breast of chicken and new rolls with the inevitable grapes in their own tissue-lined basket, and coffee; for though the day was already warming to heat it would be cool among the mountains, and Lady Vesper felt the chill.

Outside Gaston was polishing the Simca, making little crooning noises of endearment as though it was his particular pet and he could hear it preen itself.

Celeste arrived promptly at eleven. She was dressed in a yellow linen suit and looked very smart. Though she passed Hilary in the wide hall she didn't speak, and the young nurse presumed that she must be shy.

When the car had taken the picnickers off, Hilary dressed in a blue cotton dress, which was one of her personal favourites. It had frills at the neck and sleeves and another frill peeped under the hem with the suggestion of a petticoat.

She hastened down to the village where Michael Smith was, as usual, occupying a table outside the café.

He regarded her closely, without any greeting.

'Stay right there!' he commanded. 'I want to draw you.'

'Will it take long?' she asked, blushing at the compliment. 'I really haven't a lot of time, and I want my lesson.'

His charcoal pencil flashed busily.

'Two birds with one stone,' he flashed at her. 'English is *verboten* from this moment on. Struggle. It's the only way. *Travaillez!*' he insisted. '*Faites attention, maintenant.*'

For the next half hour Hilary struggled with tenses and genders and began to give quite a fair account of herself.

'You've done very well,' he told her, finally. 'It's the only way. One must jump in at the deep end and swim. Are you free for the afternoon?'

'Oh, no,' she said quickly. 'I have to keep an eye on things at the château. Verian is expected—the son. You know him?'

'I know him,' Michael said noncommittally. 'But he can take care of himself. He's had plenty of prac-

48

tice. I thought I might have taken you to see the students' exhibition of art in Aurillac. It's worth a visit.'

'I'm sorry,' Hilary said promptly.

She did not want things to get on a too-personal basis with Michael. He looked at her strangely at times; it may just have been his artist's gaze, or it may have been something deeper, and she did not intend to encourage it.

'I'm a working girl, you know,' she told him as she rose to go. 'And Lady Vesper usually means what she says. I like the drawing. What happens to it when you've finished?'

'Oh, I haven't finished with this by a long chalk. I shall maybe transfer it to canvas and finish up with a new Mona Lisa for posterity.'

'That'll be the day,' Hilary laughed lightly, and took leave of him.

She wondered if Verian would be arriving soon. If he had been driving during the night he might even reach the château in time for lunch.

She felt vaguely irritated when she noticed Dr de la Rue about to leap into the smart little Renault convertible.

'Fate, Nurse Hope!' was his greeting. 'I was about to come and get you.'

'Get me, sir?' she inquired coolly. 'Whatever for?'

'An emergency, of course. What else?'

The implication that he could only possibly need her in an emergency rankled somewhat. Unlike Michael Smith he apparently found no promise of pleasure in her company.

'What emergency, sir?' she asked.

'I have a young wife in labour. The district mid-wife has fallen downstairs and sprained her ankle and the old woman who hires herself out at such times has decided to visit her son in the next valley. Another pair of hands would be most welcome, so I thought of you.'

To her credit Hilary did not hesitate.

'If you think I can manage, certainly I'll help, Doctor. But I haven't taken my C.M.B.'

She had forgotten for the moment that he wasn't English.

'What is that?' he asked, hustling her into the cottage he had recently vacated.

'I'm not a certified midwife.'

'I suppose you know how a baby is born? That you understand the meaning of asepsis?'

'Of course, but—'

'Then titti-fa-lal for your C.M.B.s.' He pushed her inside a small, dark bathroom. 'Scrub!' he commanded. 'Then we go to work upstairs.'

A woman's urgent moaning reached Hilary as she scrubbed in milky disinfectant. Subconsciously timing the cries, she realised that the promised event was reaching a climax, and hastened up the stairs to a room where the doctor, in shirt-sleeves, flung a white overall at her.

'Better get this on,' he advised. 'We're going to have a baby any moment now.'

The girl in the bed was little more than eighteen, and Hilary gently mopped the sweat from her brow and then donned rubber gloves which de la Rue shoved at her.

'Here we go,' he said, as the girl in the bed tensed and arched once more. 'Here he comes!'

'Or she,' Hilary found time to say as a little round head appeared miraculously in her gloved hands. 'She's beautiful,' she announced as they all took a breather.

'Don't tell me that you're also a feminist, Nurse Hope? At this stage it's a boy until proved otherwise.'

'She has a girl's face,' Hilary stubbornly insisted.

'You'll make a bad midwife if you go by faces.'

At the same moment seething with resentment and glorying in the story of creation, Hilary aided a sturdy pair of shoulders into the world.

'She's a big girl,' she announced, hanging on to her end of the argument.

The rest of the birth was quick and easy. The young mother was strong and had not needed even one whiff of analgesic gas.

Raoul de la Rue looked at the baby as he cut the cord and heard its shrill cry of protest as it began its separate life. He smiled in Hilary's direction but addressed his remarks to the mother.

'Très bien, Marie! Le bébé est un fils.'

'Un fils?' the mother cried incredulously. 'Ah! Merci, le bon Dieu.'

A boy,' Raoul said quietly, as he now attended to the infant. 'With a girl's face, did you say, Nurse?'

Hilary, who was cleaning up and getting fresh linen and drawsheets from a nearby cupboard, decided to allow him his moment of triumph.

'It's a lovely baby,' she said, 'and that's really all any mother wants. Sex is unimportant except to certain mediaeval-minded men.'

'I like you, Nurse Hope,' he said, enunciating the 'h' very clearly, 'as an opposition. You make a very good opposition. When I feel like a fight I will send for you again, eh?'

'I can pass my time much more agreeably than in fighting, thank you, sir,' she said airily.

'But it is dull having everyone admire you all the time. I, too, get tired of it.'

'I'm sure everybody thinks you're wonderful,' Hilary said tartly.

'Everyone minus one, since you peek-a-boo with my bull.'

'Then it makes a refreshing change, doesn't it?'

There was the sound of voices and heavy breathing downstairs, then a man's voice calling urgently.

'*En haut, Pierre,*' Dr de la Rue invited. '*Regardez le petit beau.*'

A young man stumbled into the room wearing the clothes of an agricultural worker. His eyes sought his young wife first, and noted her proud smile of joy and fulfilment, then he looked at the scrap in her arms and fell to his knees by the bed. A middle-aged woman in the doorway, obviously the girl's mother, wept unashamedly.

'Now we go,' Dr de la Rue announced, guiding Hilary from the scene of family affection and thanksgiving. 'A clean-up and on to the rest of our muttons. I am indescribable in my thanks.'

Hilary smiled at the expression and told him she

had enjoyed every minute.

'Even to the fighting?' he wanted to know.

'Yes, even that, Doctor.'

'Good. There's hope for us, then. May I take you home to the château?'

'No, thank you. Don't bother. It's not far.'

As she walked up the long drive Hilary pondered that she really had enjoyed all her experiences of the day so far. It was now half past two and she was very hungry, rather tired, too. It would be pleasant to partake of the national habit of enjoying a siesta after lunch.

Weariness left her, however, as she saw the cream-coloured Jaguar parked in front of the house bearing G.B. plates.

Verian had obviously arrived in her absence.

She ran indoors and went straight to the dining-room. A small table near the window was set for one, she saw in some disappointment. Of course the new-comer was bound to have had lunch at this time. It was stupid to expect that he would have waited for her.

Madame Durand brought the meal in herself when Hilary rang the service bell. She appeared somewhat put out and said that soup was now *froid*.

Hilary tried out her French and explained that she had been helping the doctor to deliver a baby.

'Marie Carnet?' inquired Madame.

Hilary said she expected so, remembering Dr de la Rue had addressed the young mother as Marie. She told the woman that the child was a son, and the woman went off, burbling happily, to gossip about the news where she could.

The soup was not only *froid* but greasy as well, so Hilary left it and ate a green salad, thick with dressing, with a small piece of unidentifiable fish. After the usual grapes and coffee she wandered out on to the terrace, and then her heart leapt. There before her eyes was a green lawn and on the lawn a tall, fair young man shooting arrows at a circular target.

'Bravo!' Hilary called as he hit a bull's-eye with obvious satisfaction.

Verian Vesper glanced upwards with a bright smile which gradually died on his face. Hilary hated to admit that he was in some way disappointed at seeing her. Maybe he had expected someone else, his mother perhaps.

He climbed the steps to the terrace with a quizzical look on his handsome features, and she realised that recognition was not mutual. He had offered his hand before he said, with a triumphant note in his voice: 'You're the girl I knocked for six outside the nursing home, aren't you? Don't tell me you're Mother's new nurse!'

'All right, then, I won't,' she smiled, hiding her disappointment that he apparently knew nothing about her.

'Well, who would have thought we'd get a good-looking one eventually,' he added with heavy gallantry. 'They've all been a lot of old war-horses to date. Mother annihilates nurses as some people annihilate bugs.'

'She has already tried to annihilate me,' Hilary told him. 'But I'm surviving. She says I wear her down like water on a stone.'

'Good for you! I admire the members of your profession enormously. When I think of my mother multiplied by a thousand or so, I feel like recommending all nurses for the George Cross.'

'Your mother isn't so bad,' Hilary defended her patient. 'The trouble is she doesn't want to be nursed. I have to fight to get near her.'

'How is my mama? Or aren't you allowed to tell a member of the laity?'

'Your mother is very well within her own limits. As far as I can gather from her notes she periodically exceeds her limits.'

'How true! She hates being an invalid. It's sometimes hard on Lulu and me, too. Lulu is my sister— Louisa, to be exact.'

'How is it hard on you? You both appear to be free and flourising in your separate orbits.'

'We can't shock our parents without fearing the consequences. Lulu almost eloped with a dashing Hun once who was employed to teach her German. She learned that *'ich liebe dich'* faster than anticipated and was packed off in a Mercedes-Benz, over the border and awa,' before Interpol hauled him in for pinching the damn thing. It was then that lovelorn Lulu realised what her behaviour might have done to Mama, so she hauled down her flag and crept home, sadder and wiser.'

Hilary, not knowing whether or not to believe the story, for it was told lightly, then asked; 'Have you had to haul down *your* flag often?'

He smiled at her with half-closed blue eyes.

'If you want the story of my life you must pay a forfeit. Put on your bonnet and come for a walk.'

'With pleasure,' she said eagerly, almost too eagerly for her own peace of mind.

Lying on a pine-needle-layered slope, looking out over green woods, Hilary felt relaxed and happy in the company of a very pleasant young man. He now not only knew that she existed but liked her, she was sure, for he laughed easily at her jokes about hospital life and appeared as relaxed as she was.

'It's going to be fun having a young war-horse about the place,' he told her. 'Until Mother puts a spoke in the wheel.'

'How do you mean?'

'I mean, dear Nursie, that I'm young and you're young, male and female. By the time Mama gets around to adding it up I'll never get a minute alone with you.'

'That's surprising,' Hilary said, hoping this meant he wanted to be alone with her at times, 'because she told me to look after you when you arrived. She also said you might take me out to see the sights occasionally and that it would be nice for me. Of course, I don't intend holding your mother's suggestions like a pistol at your head. You do exactly as you please.'

'Oh, I don't know,' he bit his lower lip thoughtfully. 'If that's the way Mama wants to play it I'll string along. What's there to lose?'

He looked at Hilary for a long moment so that she felt the colour creeping up her neck and into her cheeks. He leaned towards her and she tensed as she waited to be kissed. Her heart was pounding as he merely sniffed her, however.

'I've been puzzled all afternoon by your perfume. Now I realise it isn't perfume at all, it's disinfectant.'

He picked up one of her hands and sniffed it delicately.

'Yes, it is,' her voice wobbled rather uncertainly. 'I've been helping Dr de la Rue to deliver a bouncing boy this morning. The regular midwife had sprained an ankle. I'm sorry about the smell. It sticks for days when you've had to scrub in the stuff.'

'Not to worry. It's clean and wholesome, rather typical of you in a way.'

'Thank you,' she said, somewhat wryly.

'What do you think of Raoul de la Rue?' Verian asked as they rose to walk back to the château.

'As a person or as a doctor?'

'I know he's a damn good doctor. As a person he strikes me as an intolerable bighead. How does he appear to the opposite sex?'

'Much the same, I suppose.' Hilary had an uncomfortable feeling of being disloyal to a member of her profession. She had the same diffidence when speaking critically of a patient. 'But if he's a good doctor that's all that really matters, isn't it?'

'I once thought of becoming a doctor,' Verian said. 'But de la Rue laughed in my youthfully dedicated face. He said never in a hundred years would I make the grade. I didn't, but he needn't have been so positive about it.'

'He's not all that old himself,' Hilary pondered.

'Every bit of thirty,' Verian told her seriously.

'In fact due for his pension,' she smiled, thinking he must be teasing.

'When I'm thirty', he went on, however, seriously enough, 'I shall have abandoned all hope about some things. Nine and a bit more years to go!' he sighed.

'So you're not of age yet?' she inquired.

'I shall celebrate that wonderful occasion here, in this hole, in three weeks' time. A fat lot of celebrating there'll be!'

'You mean because of your mother?'

'Yes. There'll be a quiet little do, I expect, but nothing sensational. When I think of a classical twenty-first I think of champagne coming out of a chap's ears and everybody getting ducked in the fountain. That's how it should be.'

'I spent my twenty-first on duty,' said Hilary. 'I got wonderful presents, of course, but I never did get around to having a party.'

'Well, of course it's different for people like you, isn't it?'

'You mean people of my class?' Hilary asked promptly, feeling vaguely nettled.

'I mean people who have to work for their livings don't exist on a programme of social events like we do. I know the system's all wrong, but we're caught up in it. Life should be real and earnest, but it isn't always. Mine isn't.'

Hilary was silent, so he went on: 'Don't misunderstand me, I *like* girls of your class. I really do. They're intelligent and useful.'

The breach had widened, and she wished he would drop the subject. She wasn't enjoying the walk back half as much as the journey out.

There was no 'class' in a busy hospital. There were workers and there were shirkers. The hierarchy was composed of people who had earned their promotion and their authority. Only efficiency was expected and admired.

In a well-mannered, innocent kind of way Hilary felt she had been snubbed by Verian. He was a member of 'us' and she was one of 'them'. He drew the line between them almost apologetically and immediately created a wall that was at least six foot thick and unscaleable.

She wondered if she had dreamed it all when, a moment later, he drew her arm into his and squeezed it gently.

'Maybe we can do something tomorrow? If Mother really wants us to be friends I'm already more than willing. How about it?'

She smiled and gently withdrew her arm. They were now approaching the big house from the rear.

'Of course, whenever I'm free. There's the Simca in the garage. Your mother must be back.'

She began to run, and Verian called out: 'What's the rush?'

'I'm your mother's nurse, remember,' she called over her shoulder, 'and not a house guest.'

She thought she had better remind him of this fact before things went any further between them, but she was also reminding herself that her own thoughts had been foolish at times, no matter how she had acted. Why, she had almost invited Verian to kiss her when he had had no intention of doing so. Perhaps he had noticed her excitement and quiescence and so had thought to remind her of her position.

Whatever it had been, she now felt hurt and rebuffed and so much older and wiser than the son of the house that she could have been his maiden aunt.

In her room she nursed her burning cheeks for a moment, then plunged them into cold water, after which she felt better, changed into uniform and tapped dutifully upon Lady Vesper's door.

The next week passed happily enough.

Lady Vesper's health gave no anxiety; she occasionally went for a drive and sometimes even strolled in the gardens and sat in an arbour surrounded by roses raised in and brought from Sussex.

Occasionally she had visitors, but although these were encouraged, to keep her amused and *au fait* with local gossip, Hilary had instructions from Dr de la Rue to discourage planned meetings and to shoo the callers away whenever the patient looked either tired or in any way distressed.

Whenever she could manage it Hilary took a French lesson with Michael Smith, and was coming along by leaps and bounds. She could now not only address the servants in their own language but also understand some of their responses, which sent her up very quickly in their estimation. During the afternoons, while her ladyship rested, Hilary and Verian went about together, walking, motoring or shopping. He apparently enjoyed her company, and treated her rather like a sister, with restrained affection and some teasing. He confided in her and once bared his heart.

Love, he said, was hell. He had once fallen in love, and it had threatened to muck up his whole life. It wasn't as if the girl was *anybody*.

'But I only had to see her and it was as though she held a string to my heart, and when she pulled—ooh!'

An apt description, Hilary decided, who had never been in love to such a degree.

'But you got over it!' she asked.

'I dunno. I haven't seen her lately. I've been up at Oxford slogging—I'm not brainy, so I have to slog to keep my tutors from my throat—and I may have squeezed her out. I wouldn't like to say. It was once so important to me that its very non-importance at the moment is a blessed relief. Do you understand?'

'I think so. I'm a novice myself. Don't you even write?'

'No. We decided to wait and see if it passed. Our parents were against it, in any case, which is a bit awkward when you depend on them for your pennies. She hasn't contacted me, and I promised not to pester her, so I presume she has fallen for another.'

'Sad,' signed Hilary. 'But you *are* very young.'

'So are you, Grandma, or had you forgotten the fact?'

They were sitting on a grassy hillock at the time, with Aurillac spread out like a tapestry below them.

'What would you do if I kissed you, Hilary?'

She blushed rose-red immediately.

'I really don't know. I told you, I'm a novice.'

'I'd like to see. May I?'

She wished he had just done it without asking. It made her feel foolish to agree and then wait for his mouth to descend on hers. He pressed lightly at first, then hard, and sat back, reviewing her with a new respect.

'Not at all bad,' he decided.

'What rubbish,' she said, rising in embarrassment and knowing he had been merely making an experiment. 'You kissed me to see if you had really forgotten her, and you haven't, and it shows.'

'How can you tell?' he wanted to know.

She was scraping grass from her hair and smoothing the linen skirt she was wearing.

'I'm not such a novice as all that. I've had better kisses from my labrador.'

She was glad in a way that the incident had taken place. She was no longer curious, and realised she could never be in love with Verian.

'Are you ever-so-slightly doubting my masculinity?' he demanded, mock-wrathfully.

'Take it any way you like,' she tossed over her shoulder, and began to run like a deer down the hill.

He chased her, laughing at her excited screams as he drew nearer, having longer legs. But when he caught her there was only a romp and a tussle with a great deal of laughter.

After this they were like brother and sister again, and life was pleasant and uncomplicated for a little while.

One day Lady Vesper, looking her most sweet and disarming, suddenly addressed Hilary as she was tidying away the ritual bath.

'How are you getting along with my son, Nurse?'

'Oh, very well, my lady.'

Hilary squeezed the sponge and left it draining in its rack which she had rubbed to chromium brightness.

'Good! I'm glad you've taken to one another. You're about the same age and I expect you have similar interests.'

Hilary didn't reply, but Lady Vesper's next question made her prick her ears up.

'Does he—er—see anyone else in the village?'

Thinking this somewhat odd, Hilary replied: 'I really don't know, my lady. He doesn't when he's with me. But he can tell you that himself, I expect.'

'No, it's not important, I assure you. I'm sure you're a girl with her head screwed on the right way and know how to handle young men who may imagine they're in love with you?'

This time Hilary really paid attention.

'I wouldn't know that, Lady Vesper. Not many young men have fallen in love with me recently. When they do I'll discover whether my head is screwed on the right way or not.'

In her own room she quivered with suppressed anger. In other words Lady Vesper blessed her son's friendship with the nurse so long as said nurse wasn't entertaining ideas above her station. If Verian did fall in love with her she was expected to discourage him from the outset, no matter what her own feelings might be in the matter.

'It makes me so mad,' Hilary told her reflection in

the mirror. 'To be treated as a thing rather than a person. For some reason her ladyship has handed me to Verian on a platter, but it's not for either my sake *or* his. Just what is she up to, I wonder?'

CHAPTER FOUR

LADY Vesper began to show a certain amount of interest in the young people's affairs. She pumped Hilary gently and persistently one evening while she was being prepared for bed.

'You are seeing quite a lot of my son, Nurse Hope?'

'Quite a lot, my lady.'

'You think he's attractive?'

'He *is* very good-looking. He resembles you uncannily.'

'Thank you, my dear. What a very nice compliment! Louisa is dark, you know, like her father, and she wears her hair in this floppy modern manner. Nevertheless I suppose she too is pretty, as standards go these days. She's long-legged and flat-chested. How fashions in beauty do change!'

'I suppose your late husband would have been very proud of his family now.'

Lady Vesper gave an odd little choking sound. She was laughing soundlessly.

'Whatever made you imagine my husband was "late", Nurse? He's very much alive, as a matter of fact.'

Hilary had blushed up to her eyebrows. She rarely made a *faux pas* such as this and had assumed that Sir William Vesper had died. They must be divorced or something, and if it had been an unhappy affair it was most careless on her part to revive painful memories.

'I'm sorry, my lady,' she said sincerely. 'I didn't know.'

'Now you're sorry he's alive, eh? Naughty Nurse!' Lady Vesper was still teasing, thank heaven! 'Actually we're merely separated for our mutual benefit, nothing official. An invalid wife is a great drag upon a man whose instincts are to spend the best part of the year shooting big game for film companies or climbing impossible mountains. When I found I couldn't cope with it I took the leash off and let him go. The result is he's actually very much attached to me and sees me so infrequently as never to become acutely aware of my failings. So what do you think of that for an arrangement, eh?'

'I think you made a very brave decision, Lady Vesper. I'm sure I couldn't have done it.'

'Rubbish! I used my noddle. When you have a useless heart like mine something else has to work overtime. I'm a human calculating machine, and don't ever forget it.'

'I won't.' Hilary promised with a smile.

'And what do you and my son do together?'

'Oh, we walk, and talk. He's making a toxophilite out of me.'

'That's a very good word! Do you make love?'

'No, we don't.' Hilary was glad she could answer that one quite honestly.

'Oh. I thought nowadays young people were quite free with that sort of thing.'

'Not all young people,' Hilary told her. 'Verian and I are quite happy on a platonic plane.'

This appeared to give Lady Vesper food for thought.

'Does he see anyone else when you're out? I mean —other girls?'

'Not that I know of,' Hilary sounded her surprise at the question.

'I'm really not prying,' the woman said quickly. 'It's just that, with a boy as attractive as my son, girls sometimes get ideas above themselves. He's at an impressionable age.'

'I'm sure he has good sense and taste,' Hilary said, thinking to reassure the other.

'He hadn't the good sense to fall in love with you, had he?' her ladyship countered with a full broadside. 'It may have done him a lot of good and got some other poison out of his system. Nothing works out the way one wants it to. You I could have handled.'

Hilary gathered from this that Lady Vesper would have condoned a mild flirtation between her son and her nurse, but nothing more serious. In fact she appeared somewhat put out because they had not gone to the limit of her expectations. The girl didn't quite like or understand that bit about handling, but thought it to mean that after she had served her purpose and kept Verian interested in her for a little while, she could then be disposed of without any great trouble on her ladyship's part.

Now she began to respect the woman for her calculating machine of a mind, but was relieved to think that opportunity had not really involved her in any intrigues.

The next morning she practised archery with Verian and even scored an inner, though not a bull's-eye. The sport was not active enough for him today, however, and seizing her hand he said: 'Let's go down to the village. I want a walk.'

'And I need another French lesson.' She had told him about the arrangement with Michael, which he approved.

Michael was not at the rendezvous, however, and Hilary wondered what could be amiss. He had promised to lend her some books, today, and made her promise to come early as he was going into Aurillac later in the morning.

'I think I'll just wander round to the *pension* where he stays,' Hilary told her companion. 'You have a coffee while I'm gone.'

'*Monsieur Smees est malade*,' the woman who kept the *pension* told her. '*Tres malade*.'

Hilary asked if she might see him, and was shown up to a room at the very top of the house. It was practically papered with drawings and untidy with artists' paraphernalia. She could only reach the bed in the darkest corner with difficulty and saw that Michael was shivering and had a fever.

'I get malaria,' he told her. 'That's all it is. Malaria.'

She felt his head. It was raging.

'That's nice,' he said. 'You've got cool, cool hands. I love you, Hilary. You know that? I'm awfully in love with you.'

She decided it was the fever talking and asked if he had seen the doctor.

'I've got no money for doctors. It costs money to be ill here. I'll get over it. I always do.'

'You're having the doctor this time, Michael, and I won't hear any argument against it. You haven't charged me a penny for my lessons and I'm deeply in your debt. I'll pay the doctor's bills.'

Without listening to his protests, and he was really far too ill to insist, she left the room and told Madame she was going to telephone the doctor. In less than half an hour Raoul de la Rue arrived and heard the story.

'The English always amaze me,' he said when he heard of Michael's anxiety about the expense. 'I really think they enjoy physical endurance. It makes them feel stronger than anybody else. Did you ever hear of any doctor who threatened "your money or your life"? Ridiculous young man!'

An hour had sped before Hilary returned to the café, and she scarcely expected Verian still to be there. But he was, and he was not alone. The girl Celeste was with him, and the two were so engrossed in one another that they didn't notice her approach.

'Hello!' she announced herself.

Verian looked up with a start and then stood, as good manners demanded. His eyes looked chill, however.

'I think you two know one another?' he enquired.

'Yes, we have met.' Hilary nodded in Celeste's direction and the other girl smiled, not a friendly smile but one almost of triumph.

Verian saluted the French girl, whispered something in her ear which made her laugh and blush at the same time, and then hustled Hilary away from the scene as though anxious to come to grips with her.

'Why didn't you tell me Celeste was up at the house the day I arrived? Why did she imagine you were my—my fiancée? Whatever gave her that idea?'

Hilary had had a busy and tiring hour and rather resented his tone.

'I don't know what you're talking about. I didn't know you knew the girl, and my French was not up to telling her I was anything of the sort. I hadn't even met you the day she came and went out with your mother. Whatever she presumed was none of my doing. I'm not ashamed of my calling or being known for what I am, your mother's nurse.'

'Ah, of course it would be Mother's doing,' he said thoughtfully. 'She probably used you to try and frighten Celeste off. She's a devil. Just imagine, I could have been seeing Celeste every day, and neither of us knew the other was within a hundred miles of the château, thanks to my dear mama.'

'You mean—' Hilary was aghast—'that Celeste is the girl you were in love with?'

'I was, and now I believe I still am. She feels the same way. Mother took her on that picnic and gave her to understand I wasn't expected this summer. She also told her you were my present girlfriend.'

'So that's why she told me to change out of uniform,' Hilary mused. 'And although I didn't understand what they were saying to one another, Celeste was giving me the blackest of looks. Why does your mother object to your friendship? She's a very pretty girl.'

Verian laughed cynically.

'You must have discovered by this that my mother is a terrible snob. I suppose Lulu and I are almost as bad, because of the things which she has always impressed on us. People are either right or wrong for us to know; right by virtue of birth, not by either beauty or intellect. Celeste is wrong because she's the daughter of a vet descended from a farmer; she's studying at a veterinary college to become an animal nurse and to assist her father. People who have to work for their livings are wrong people, unless they do it for fun, like debs and modelling. I don't know how nurses stand with her. Nursing is a profession, isn't it?'

'I'll tell you how they stand,' Hilary said with some show of spirit. 'They're all right for a flirtation just so long as they have no mistaken ideas about becoming a member of the exalted family. If your mother wasn't the way she is I would like to tell her a few home truths; that even the 'wrong' people have hearts and feelings one can hurt. We're not living in feudal times now, and the sooner Lady Vesper realises that, the better for all concerned.'

They walked up the long drive to the house in silence, then Verian stopped and pulled Hilary round to face him.

'Don't tell mother I've seen Celeste. You will see, now, what a bind it's always been for Lulu and me to conform when she's so dictatorial and sly—and yet so

71

delicate in health. I firmly believe a chap has to pick his own wife, however, and I'll decide about Celeste for myself. You won't tell her?'

'Of course not. I'm not her spy. I'd better go now, and see if she wants anything.'

Lady Vesper was comfortably reading the mail which had just arrived, however. She looked as innocent as a babe as she re-read a letter in her hands.

'Isn't that sweet? William is trying to come to St Jude for Verian's coming-of-age. It will be so nice to see him again!' She sighed. 'I don't care what anybody says, we must have a nice big party and invite everybody who *is* anybody. You shall come too, Nurse. Wouldn't you like to dance under coloured lights on the terrace with Verian?'

'That would be very nice,' Hilary responded, and my lady apparently didn't notice that her nurse's tone was just fractionally sarcastic.

· CHAPTER FIVE

AFTER the abnormalities of Lady Vesper and her intrigues, Hilary found it a relief to relax after lunch with the normal outpourings of her family and friends. Lassie, the labrador, had given birth to four pups, two golden and two black. Mrs Hope took an interest in breeding thoroughbreds and had decided to keep one of the bitches for Lassie's sake and to breed from her later on. 'So think up a good name for the new pet,' she told her daughter. 'You are usually the most inspired about such things.'

Hilary began to turn names over in her mind immediately. She had named Lassie, very grandly, 'Hopeful Harriet of Thatchdown', Thatchdown being the name of their house where Lassie had been born of their old, now deceased, jet labrador. 'Hopeful Harriet' became Lassie within a few days, however, and that was the way it would be with the new pup.

'Hopeful Hildegarde?' Hilary tried out, but decided that was too top-heavy. 'I could call her after me, "Hopeful Hilary of Thatchdown," but it sounds too much like a disappointed old maid. Anyway, perhaps that's what I'll become. Verian didn't find me desperately attractive, did he?'

She reviewed the situation with a vague sensation of depression. She felt guilty about feeling depressed while on holiday, and also she foresaw that now Verian and Celeste had rediscovered one another, despite her ladyship's plots to foil their meeting, the son of the house would no longer require her company for his amusement.

'The trouble is,' Hilary decided, 'that I have too much time to think of such things and not enough work to do. I don't want Lady Vesper to be ill, but even she doesn't seem to need me. She suffers my ministrations but probably thinks them a bore.'

There was a letter from Cathy, so she decided to read it and cheer herself up.

'—And what exactly are you up to?' Cathy asked darkly. 'I hear those Frenchmen are devastating with their hand-kissing and what-not . . . '

Hilary paused to ponder that the only two men in her life at St Jude were both English: Verian and Michael. There seemed to be no interesting young men in the village. Probably they all sought the big cities as soon as they were old enough to flee their homes.

The picture of a haughty countenance with deep-set grey eyes and aquiline nose flashed across her mind's eye and she quickly shook it away.

'*He* doesn't count,' she told herself. 'He sees me as an extra hand, occasionally, and that's all. He's probably married, anyway, with half a dozen children. I must ask Verian, if he can spare me a moment.'

' . . . Things here are much the same,' Cathy proceeded, 'with the usual gossip which, if half of it were true, would more than fill the *News of the World*. That red-headed nurse on Maternity was suspended on being caught in the linen-cupboard with a doctor, who shall be nameless. Remember, kiddo, it's the woman who always pays in our profession. Never look at a doctor unless he's proposed to you in front of witnesses. They're a dangerous breed, and so darned attractive. I don't know what makes them so . . .'

'Yes, I suppose he *is* attractive,' Hilary once more paused to ponder. 'He could be devastating if he really tried.'

' . . . so life goes on,' Cathy concluded. 'Drinkies and bikkies and potties and beddies. One really talks like that after a while on my ward. I believe when we're taken off we're automatically certified and transferred to the head-shrinkers for the next six months. I miss you, Hilary, and oh, how I envy you! How about a swop?'

Hilary smiled as she pocketed her letters. She envied Cathy the hospital. There was really no satisfying anybody.

The afternoon dragged, somehow. Verian was about his own business and didn't once appear to ask what she was doing. She had become so used to his attentiveness that she really missed him. She talked in halting French with one of the gardeners for a while, and though he understood her perfectly, which pleased her, she couldn't altogether follow his responses, and, like most Frenchmen, he seemed to say far more than was necessary to the conversation. She eventually drifted to a lounging chair and opened a book. The sun was hot, but a canvas awning protected her head, and after watching a cobweb of cloud drift slowly across the heavens, she laid down the book and closed her eyes for a moment.

An hour later a hand gently shook her.

'Verian!' she called out gladly, but it wasn't Verian, it was Dr de la Rue, and he was smiling wryly. He called every day at the château, mostly in the afternoons.

'Naughty girl!' he scolded her. 'Your legs will be burnt.'

'No,' she denied, although they were stinging a bit even now. 'I'm very tough, and I want to look as though I've been in the sun, sir.'

'Why do you call me "sir"?' he asked. 'I am not a schoolmaster.'

'We do in England.'

'I ought to know that. My mother is English and I was born in London.'

'Were you, sir?' she asked politely.

'But not to change the subject. This is not England and the sun is very hot for an English rose. Remember that, in future.'

Hilary had never thought of herself as an English rose before. She was subtly flattered.

'All English girls have delicate skins, blonde or brunette,' he told her, shattering the illusion that he had meant to please by his remark. 'I thought you might like to know about the young man, your friend . . . '

'Verian?' she asked promptly.

'No, not Verian. The young man with the fever.'

'Oh, Michael! How is he?'

'Very much better. The young idiot has responded

to mepacrine like a charm. I have left him a supply of tablets for future use, and I will not send him a bill for my services.'

'Oh, I'll pay,' Hilary offered eagerly.

'I wouldn't take your money,' Dr de la Rue said unequivocally. 'What is he to you, this young man?'

'He's been helping me with my French, that's all.'

'When he was rambling he said—well, I gathered he was more than attached to you.'

'Feverish people do say things they would rather not remember when they are well, Doctor. I've never encouraged Michael Smith in any way whatsoever.'

'You prefer Verian?'

'I'm not serious about Verian, either. We're friends, that's all.'

'You are annoyed with me. I pry too much, eh, little one? But I am relieved you do not think too much of Master Verian Vesper. He is so very, very young and inadequate, not at all suitable for an intelligent girl like you.'

Though she felt flattered once more, Hilary couldn't resist asking: 'And has intelligence ever been known to have any bearing upon falling in love, sir?'

'No,' he smiled broadly. 'But one always has the hope. Now shall we go up and see our patient?'

'She is disgustingly healthy, this one,' Dr de la Rue decided as he examined Lady Vesper in his usual thorough manner. 'So much improved. Not trying to run when she must walk. I think, perhaps, Nurse Hope is good for you, Caroline?'

'Perhaps,' the woman said blandly. 'She certainly doesn't antagonise me like some of those dreadful old gorgons I've had in the past. Sometimes I pretend she isn't there at all, she's so unobtrusive. She makes a nice sensible companion for Verian.'

The man glanced at Hilary; his eyebrows were two question-marks. 'I shouldn't think *I* should find Nurse nice and sensible, if I were a young man.'

Hilary flushed once again and pretended to be busy, as though she didn't know they were talking about her.

'Oh, come, Raoul. You're not as ancient as all that. Ever since that business with Yvonne you've behaved like your own grandfather. You're still a young man and it's time you realised it. I hate to see youth and vitality thrown away on the dead.'

Dr de la Rue's stethoscope was pocketed. He didn't speak as he packed up his things.

'I haven't offended you, surely, Raoul?' asked Lady Vesper, just a little anxiously.

'No, no, of course not. How can *you* offend anyone, dear lady?'

Hilary felt that the question was double-edged. Lady Vesper was so practised she could offend without really trying. It appeared that Raoul de la Rue had had a wife, or a sweetheart, named Yvonne, who had died. Hilary felt sorry for him having to suffer her name dragged up in public like this, and then dismissed with a shrug of the shoulders as being of no further importance.

He pulled himself together with an effort.

'Can you spare your nurse for an hour or so, Caroline? I have someone who wants to see her.'

'Well, of course,' Lady Vesper said, a little dubiously nevertheless. She liked to direct other people's activities, not to have them taken out of her hands. 'Not too late, Nurse. Remember my massage.'

Hilary went next door to change. She donned a yellow dress which was one of her favourites and she hadn't yet worn it. Why she should put it on now she couldn't imagine, but perhaps she had some idea of cheering Dr de la Rue up with her own appearance.

He scarcely glanced at her, as she joined him at his car which Gaston had been polishing while they were indoors.

'Where are we going?' she asked. 'Who wants to see me? I scarcely know anyone.'

'Perhaps you make all the greater impact on the few you do know, Hill-ary. Do you mind if I call you Hill-ary?'

'Not at all, sir.' She didn't make the mistake of addressing him as Raoul. A doctor was a doctor, after all, and could afford to unbend a little to his subordinates. The reverse was not the case, however.

'Where we are going is a surprise. You will see.'

The car stopped in the straggling high street of the village, opposite the house where Hilary had helped bring a baby into the world. The little boy with a girl's face, she now smiled to remember.

Raoul de la Rue took her arm and drew her through the house to where a courtyard opened out at the back. There were a great many people in the courtyard, all drinking wine and making merry. In one corner, in the shade, was a wooden crib, obviously an antique, and in it lay the baby, his skin now pale and his expression serene. Only a week or so ago he had been as red as a beetroot and quite cross about his entry into the world.

'Oh, he's sweet!' Hilary said, with that peculiar lump in her throat which comes to most women when they behold the wonder of the human child.

All round the crib and on it were packages of various shapes and sizes. The significance of these suddenly dawned on the girl and she turned to Raoul de la Rue in some embarrassment.

'I didn't know. I haven't got anything to give the baby.'

He looked upon her suddenly very kindly.

'But you have got something, Hill-ary,' he told her seriously. 'Your name. The parents are so grateful for your help they wish to call their son after you. Behold! *La petit Hilaire.*'

Hilary was laughing and crying all at the same time. She put a hand to her lashes and shook her head to clear her eyes.

'Please excuse me. I'm so flattered. I never had anything as nice as this happen to me before.'

Dr de la Rue squeezed her free hand encouragingly as the young parents came from a cluster of relatives to greet them.

'Then may it not be your last,' he whispered, and thrust his big white handkerchief at her with an injunction for her to 'Blow!'

During the next few days Hilary found out a good deal about Dr Raoul de la Rue, for he made a point of asking her to accompany him down to his car after he had paid his visit to Lady Vesper, and as they walked downstairs and across the wide hall they chatted, less and less about their patient and more and more about themselves.

They usually had so much to say that they strolled very slowly indeed across the terrace and descended the wide marble steps almost *tête-à-tête*.

Hilary no longer found him arrogant and unapproachable, and she was glad of these few minutes' companionship, for Verian continued to be occupied in other ways and she rarely saw him apart from meal-times.

Thus, as she confided her fears that her recent illness may have interfered with her career more than she cared to think, he told her of his own problems. He had taken over his father's practice after the old man's death two years ago, and this had interfered with his plans for specialising in paediatrics. Why did he not put a locum in charge of the practice and continue with his plans? Hilary asked him. He replied that there was not only a busy, sprawling practice to consider but a widowed mother and a considerable family estate to maintain.

'An only son is expected to be the stay and support of Mama, run the practice *and* be farm manager. That way all is much more economical. You must come and see my mother, Nurse Hope. She is English. Did I tell you? Do not think I am—what is it—griping? I am happy. Also I scheme and plan.

Here in this healthy place I build a convalescent home for sick children one of these days. That is my dream. The best of both worlds, you call it?'

'I think that's a wonderful dream,' Hilary said sincerely. 'And I certainly hope it comes true.'

'It will. Things do if you want them badly enough.'

He looked at her as he said this, and she saw that his fine grey eyes were filled with a burning enthusiasm.

He told her not to worry about her health or her job.

'I am sure they are not putting you off with excuses or thinking that there is anything really wrong with you that these few extra weeks of light duties won't put right. I would have been told, otherwise, and I assure you I have no secrets. Providing you take no chills you should soon be one hundred per cent fit.' He looked at her with those disconcertingly clear eyes of his. 'You look very healthy to me, and as pretty as a true Parisienne.'

She blushed and laughed at the unexpected compliment.

'Well, thank you, sir. I take it that you don't think the English are pretty in their own right?'

'Well—er—yes, in a plums and custard way, perhaps.'

'Don't you mean peaches and cream?' she twinkled.

'I knew it was some kind of dessert. All the time I torment my mama with my foul English. She is so ashamed of me. Or do I do it to tease, do you think?'

He left her without answering his own question,

left her smiling, for she had enjoyed their chat. She felt that so far their conversational gambits were mere scratches on the surface of great unplumbed depths of both wisdom and wit. Whereas there was little of Verian, both his conversation and his character, that remained mysterious to her after their short acquaintance, she felt she hadn't even begun to know Raoul de la Rue, and almost half her stay at the château was over. There simply wouldn't be time to get to know him much better even providing that he was sufficiently interested in her to welcome their closer association.

One day she was settling Lady Vesper for her afternoon nap. Her ladyship had a headache and had taken some tablets, when Verian sauntered into the room.

'Hullo, Mother! Hilary . . . '

'Hullo!' Hilary responded automatically.

Lady Vesper looked from one to the other.

'Have you two young things had a tiff?' she wanted to know.

'Why, no—' Verian had flushed uncomfortably, so it was Hilary who answered.

'Why should you think that, my lady?'

'I thought you were being cool with one another.'

'Rubbish!' Verian recovered sufficiently to say.

It wasn't so personal a thing as coolness, Hilary decided, it was simply disinterest.

'Is he giving you a good time, Nurse? Showing you all the sights, as I suggested?'

Feeling Verian's eyes boring into her back, Hilary spoke without hesitation.

'Verian has been very kind to me, Lady Vesper. He has shown me many things and places. Now you must rest and let the tablets have effect. Would you mind leaving your mother to sleep if she can, Verian?'

'No, not at all.'

He trailed out of the room on her heels.

'You were a sport not to give me away,' he said gratefully. 'Thanks.'

'Give you away?' she echoed. 'I simply spoke the truth.'

'In the past tense. Verian *has been* very kind to me. Not *is being*. I'm sorry if I've neglected you just lately, Hilary.'

'That's quite all right, Verian. You're not my keeper.'

'I hope you understand? Perhaps I should explain . . .'

'No! For goodness' sake don't do that. What I don't know I can't tell, can I?'

'But you *do* know I've met Celeste again. You saw us. I shall burst if I don't confide in somebody. Where *are* you dashing off to now, Hilary?'

'I'm going down to the kitchen to boil my hypodermics. Come on with me if you want to talk.'

Celeste, he told her, was at present blowing hot and then cold with him.

'At first she said it was all still the same. Then she started quoting some of the people at her wretched veterinary college and made me feel like a twit. She says she's grown up a great deal during the past year, but that I have not. How d'you like that? I love her,

Hilary, and I'm desperate.'

'I don't think I'm qualified to advise you,' the girl said dubiously. 'Only as a woman. Why don't you talk to Dr de la Rue? He knows you both.'

'Because I know what he would say—the same thing he said about my doctoring, that I haven't the faintest hope of being a great lover, either. What do *you* say. That interests me more.'

'I think you're too young, Verian, to be sure of yourself. Possibly Celeste feels this, too. We can't ignore the fact that girls do mature much earlier. You and I are practically the same age, but I feel like an elderly aunt when you appeal to me like this. I frankly don't think this love of yours will stand the test of time; I also know you will want to find that out for yourself. Still, there *is* plenty of time. Don't rush into anything.'

'Has Mother been at you.'

'Of course not.' There was a sharpness in Hilary's tone.

'Sorry! I can't help but feel that her spies are everywhere, perhaps influencing Celeste against me. Would you like to go out with me somewhere to-morrow? I would like to make up to you for my neglect of the past few days. After all, I found you a good little scout. I enjoyed those excursions of ours. No complications, not like now.'

She smiled as she relented.

'Where do you suggest we go?' she asked.

'Somewhere pastoral and peaceful. Le Lac des Chevaux. You'll like it. We can bathe there.'

'It sounds delightful.'

'Good! Now come on with me down to the village for a walk. It'll do us both good.'

She felt glad that he was apparently taking an interest in her company again. He squeezed her hand chummily on occasion and made little grimaces of pleasure at her to which she reacted reciprocally.

'Where are we going?' she inquired in surprise as he pulled her to a halt outside Michael's lodging.

'I thought we'd call and see how your friend is today.'

Hilary had kept herself *au fait* with Michael's progress through Dr de la Rue. He was progressing satisfactorily.

'He's not my friend, you know,' she said promptly, though this sounded rather churlish and she added, 'not in the way that people are inclined to couple a man and woman in friendship. But we can see how he is if you like.'

Michael was resting on an old cane lounging chair in the courtyard behind the house, but he was obviously glad to have visitors.

They spoke of one thing and another, and finally Verian said: 'You know, this lad needs a quick pick-me-up. I wonder if he would care to accompany us to the lake tomorrow, Hilary?'

Because he had addressed her and not Michael she had to answer first.

'I wonder,' she echoed, giving Verian a very meaning look. 'Would you care for a trip out tomorrow, Michael?'

'Well, thanks. You're sure I won't be *de trop*?'

'Not at all, old chap,' Verian said easily. 'We'll

make it a foursome, and that will be very nice all round.'

Hilary controlled herself until they were well clear of the *pension*, and then she let fly at her companion.

'Of all the rotten tricks, Verian! You don't have to take me out, you know, or find a companion for me. I'm very well able to keep myself entertained and choose my own friends. I don't care for having Michael Smith thrust on me willy-nilly. I had already decided to keep our acquaintance on a strictly impersonal basis.'

'I thought he was a nice enough fellow.'

'Nice enough for a simple girl like me, you mean, your mother's little nurse?'

'You're really ratty, aren't you, Hilary? I'm sorry. I really had meant it just to be you and me, and then when I saw him looking all peaky I thought it would do him good and I could ask Celeste along. I really think she would like a foursome better.'

'I'm beginning to believe you think of nobody but yourself, Verian. I shall go along tomorrow so as not to disappoint Michael, but after this please leave me out of your schemes. Now I'm sure you want to inform Celeste that you've managed to raise a party to go on this excursion, so I can find my own way back to the house.'

'I say Hilary, you *are* a sport.'

She looked at him in utter bewilderment. He didn't recognise sarcasm if it suited his ends not to, and really thought everyone else was a pawn where his own desires were concerned, to be moved hither and thither at will.

She was not looking forward to the morrow at all now, and felt even less enthusiastic when she saw Dr de la Rue just leaving the house.

She waved his car to a stop, sorry that she had missed him.

'Any instructions, Dr?' she asked.

'Yes, Nurse. Wear a hat in the sun,' he advised her kindly, and with a nod set the car in motion again.

She looked after him thoughtfully.

'Don't get involved there,' she advised herself, 'or you'll only get hurt. Watch out, Hilary! He doesn't really see you at all, whereas you're beginning to see him as someone larger than life.'

CHAPTER SIX

HILARY was miserably conscious, as she struck out in the mountain cool water of the Lac des Chevaux, a private lake in the beautiful grounds of a ruined château about twelve miles from St Jude, that nobody was really enjoying themselves on this excursion.

During the car ride when Celeste had sat in the front seat alongside Verian and Hilary had been self-consciously aware of Michael regarding her rather than the scenery in the back, the car driver was obviously put out and sulky by something his supposed girl friend had said to him. After a couple of miles Celeste turned and forced herself upon Michael in a conversation pointedly carried on in French. Hilary now found herself able to understand quite a lot, though she wasn't addressed by the other girl, who had never quite forgiven her for having been introduced as a girl-friend of Verian's and she heard Celeste remind Michael that they had met the previous summer during the battle of the flowers in Aurillac. Michael gallantly said that he did remember, that he had sketched her from her place on a decorated float and had great difficulty finding the right tonal shade of her dark red hair. This obviously pleased Celeste, who simpered and smirked, while Verian almost drove them into the back of a tanker because he wasn't concentrating on his job.

During their picnic lunch, overlooking the lake, Celeste had again monopolised Michael while Verian obviously seethed and had not the grace to talk to Hilary and ensure that she was not left out of things. She was somewhat wryly amused by the way his plot to make a twosome into a foursome had recoiled on his own head and really couldn't sympathise with him. He was a young man who had usually had his own way in everything without much difficulty, and now that Celeste had been assured that she had no rival for his affections she appeared less enthusiastic over her conquest than previously.

Hilary didn't feel particularly drawn to Celeste, for she was a girl who appeared to find more pleasure in masculine company and didn't hesitate to show her preference.

Now, after a rest for digestion in the sun, they were swimming and trying to sound more carefree than they were.

'Come on, Michael!' Hilary called. 'I'll race you to the island.'

They struck out and crawled out on the green patch of dry land panting and laughing. Hilary was a strong swimmer, but was surprised by her own tiredness after the short sprint.

'I—I'm out of condition,' she gasped. 'And my, the water's cold!'

'Straight from the top,' Michael explained, pointing towards the purple shadow of the high *massif*. 'But invigorating.' He nodded towards Verian and Celeste, who were disporting themselves in the shallows. 'What's up with those two?'

'The growing pains of love,' Hilary explained. 'Now they know one another better it isn't all as wonderful as they had thought.'

'I—er—thought you had a thing about that young man,' Michael said slyly.

'Me? No. Whatever gave you that idea?'

'I've gathered that you were putting up a "keep off the grass" sign for my benefit.'

'Not at all.'

'Then,' he reached out for her hand suddenly, urgently, and gripped it tightly, 'ever since I saw you, Hilary, I've thought of no girl but you. Honestly. I don't earn a lot, but things will improve, and—'

'Please, Michael,' she released herself in some embarrassment, 'I've never led you to think that I regarded you as anything but a tutor who became a friend. Verian means nothing to me, but I didn't say there wasn't someone else . . .'

'Oh! You mean you're engaged?'

'No, I'm not anything. In fact he's barely aware of my existence, but that doesn't stop me feeling the way I do.'

'Oh, again! Well, I hope it works out all right for you, better than it did for me,' he added bitterly.

'Michael, you scarcely know me,' she told him. 'It's this climate, or something, and everybody thinks they're in love with everybody else. We'll probably all wake up when we get back home and realise how foolish we've been.'

'This other chap you mentioned. Do I know him?'

She blushed up to her eyebrows.

'I'm not telling you, Michael. You shouldn't ask me that.'

She was not putting him off with even the whitest of white lies. Lying there under the blue bowl of the summer sky she had seen very clearly the vision of only one who could honestly match up to all her requirements in the name of true love, and it was with an aching heart that she acknowledged the fact that he would not be thinking of her in the same way, if at all.

'Let's go back to the others,' she suggested, feeling suddenly self-conscious in Michael's company.

In a way she was glad the situation had arisen between them and been dealt with. It had been hovering like a cloud for some time now.

Another hour dragged with Celeste and Verian arguing about whether they should explore the colourful gardens of the château or investigate the nearby town. It finished with them doing neither, for the purple of the moutains suddenly descended upon them with all the promise of a sudden storm.

'We should go back,' Hilary suggested uneasily. 'The road wasn't too good in parts, and if there's heavy rain it may be difficult for you, Verian.'

'I am just beginning to enjoy myself,' Celeste said arbitrarily, in quite passable English. 'I think you are afraid of storms, Nurse 'Ope?'

'Not at all, but I promised to be back by four-thirty. I *am* a working girl, after all.'

'Come on, then,' Verian said, leading the way to the car as the first flash of lightning zig-zagged across the dark sky.

The rain came ten minutes later, in sheets, and Celeste squealed as they tore through it, getting soaked.

'Stop! Verian! Put up ze 'ood.'

He hurtled on, defying her.

'Verian,' Hilary leaned across to say, her hair plastered to her neck, 'is there any need for us to get soaked?'

Without a word he stopped the car and he and Michael struggled to put up the hood manually, the mechanism of this operation having failed.

'I 'ate you!' Celeste was dancing in the rain, looking like a water-nymph. 'You do eet on ze purpose!'

'Oh, shut up! We're all wet, not just you.'

When they got into the car once more Hilary handed Celeste a spare towel which had kept dry in its plastic container. The French girl almost wept in gratitude as she dried her face and hair and then draped the towel round her shoulders.

'What about you?' she asked, belatedly.

'It's all right. We're nearly home now.'

They were sitting beside one another, the two men having gravitated together.

'Zat was most kind of you, 'ilary.'

'Not at all. Glad to be of service.'

But Hilary was shivering by the time Verian deposited her at the Château des Bois, having dropped the others first. It was unfortunate that she should run into Dr de la Rue on the stairs, of all people.

'What is the meaning of this?' he demanded, looking from her to Verian. 'Is this the way you bathe, without undressing?'

'Very funny,' said Verian, bad-temperedly, and marched on his way, leaving a damp trail in his wake.

'We came through a storm,' she explained, her teeth chattering. 'With this result.'

'Very fitting for a post-pneumonia subject,' he said scathingly. 'Go immediately into a hot bath and then to bed. I'll call to see you a little later.'

She felt like a small girl who had just been spanked as she went along to the bathroom which had been allotted to her use—there were four bathrooms on this floor—and peeled off her clothes in relief. She soaked in hot water for half an hour and then topped it off with a cold shower. By the time she had put on her uniform she felt so much better that she decided to carry on as though nothing had happened and went in to see Lady Vesper. Her ladyship had enjoyed a very pleasant day and wanted to talk about it. Raoul, dear, considerate Raoul, had taken her for a walk to the Italian garden. She hadn't seen the Italian garden for years as it was about a quarter of a mile from the house. They had walked very slowly and rested frequently, and even now she wasn't at all tired.

'I feel quite a sense of achievement. I'm better, Nurse. It must be all those massages, eh?'

'They do help,' Hilary agreed, falling in with her patient's happy mood. 'I'm so glad you were able to see the Italian garden. Verian showed it to me one day and it really is beautiful at this time of year. But having achieved so much I must insist that you rest now, and live to repeat your triumph. I'll help you into bed.'

'My dear little dictator! But I won't argue, for once, as I feel well content. Did you have a pleasant trip?'

'We did until a thunderstorm crept upon us, and then I'm afraid we all got very wet.'

'*All* of you?' My lady was suddenly watchful. 'Who went along, then, besides you and my son?'

Hilary thought very quickly.

'An Englishman, who stays every summer in the village, and his girl-friend. Michael has had a bout of malaria, so Verian suggested the trip might do him good.'

'I see.'

Hilary hoped she might be forgiven for keeping Celeste's name out of things. In her present happy mood it would be a pity to disturb Lady Vesper's evening with news of that affair.

She was glad that the subject was tacitly dropped and went off to get her evening meal. Verian was not in the dining-room, and Madame Durand informed her that he had asked for a tray to be taken to his room.

'Maybe he has caught a chill,' Hilary pondered. 'I must go along and see him later.'

Just as the storm was gathering itself up for a further onslaught over the Bois, Raoul de la Rue arrived, breathing fire. He came the length of the dining-room with a darkling brow.

'Nurse Hope, I thought I told you to have a bath and go straight to bed?'

'Well, I felt all right and so I carried on,' she said defensively.

'Nurse Hope,' each word was a whiplash now, 'I am not used to having my advice disregarded. I thought you had some small concern for your own health, and I too was prepared to guard it to the extent of my professional ability. I don't care if you feel like climbing Everest, you will go to your bed this instant and give me an opportunity of examining you properly. I shall give you five minutes to pander to my foolish whim and that is all.'

She found herself scurrying away to do his bidding, stopping in the doorway to say: 'I think it's Verian you ought to see. He didn't feel like coming down to dinner.'

He frowned so darkly that she disappeared without further argument.

'How can I have imagined myself in love with him when he's so hateful?' she asked herself as she undressed in her small room. 'He makes me feel so small and stupid at times, and nobody ever did that to me before.'

The next day Hilary had developed a running cold, so Dr de la Rue kept her in bed for forty-eight hours. He came himself to give Lady Vesper her injection, and was cool and efficient in his dealings with his newest patient.

'I feel a fool,' she complained, 'staying in bed with a mere sniffle.'

'Better to feel a fool at this stage than an idiot if it should descend to your chest again, my dear girl. Just do as you are told and we will all be happy.'

Verian called in to see her, carrying a peace-offering of red roses, wonderfully scented.

'I say,' he complained, 'de la Rue tore the most awful strip off me because I let you get wet. I didn't know you were delicate.'

'I'm not. But I did have pneumonia, and he's being an old woman about it. I feel so awful because I'm supposed to be looking after your mother, not lying here being waited on hand and foot myself. I would get up, but he would be so scathing when he found out.'

'You're telling me! He made me feel about six when he got on his high horse a little while ago. I don't deserve to hold a driving licence or have charge of other people, so he says, until I can learn to look after myself properly, which doesn't seem to be an eventuality likely to take place in the immediate future. I want to grow up, he urged, which is not to be confused with simply getting older. Just who does he think he is?'

Hilary smiled wryly, but made no reply.

'Thanks for the flowers,' she said eventually. 'They're glorious. Is—er—everything all right again between you and Celeste?'

'So-so,' he hedged. 'She's coming to my do next week.'

'Of course, your twenty-first celebration. Who's taking care of the arrangements?'

'Lulu, I expect. Girls like that sort of thing. Mother will put her oar in and Father will foot the bill. I would much rather sneak off to Lyons with Celeste than face a mob, but the son and heir's coming-of-age is a bit of a lark for a family, I expect.'

'I like that "heir" bit. Do you expect to come into money?'

'My grandfather left a trust for me. Nobody can keep it away from me any longer. I not only get the key of the door but the key to a bank vault as well. I'll be really worth knowing after next week, Hilary. Are you interested?'

'I don't think a fortune would sway me in anybody's favour, personally, but if that's a backhanded proposal I promise to consider it in the light of your coming prospects.'

They both laughed.

'I really do like you, Hilary,' Verian said softly, sitting on the side of the bed and taking her hand in his. 'You're fresh, like that,' he pointed to an unfurling rosebud which she had been admiring. 'Why can't the girl one loves be as nice as you?'

'Perhaps she is, really,' Hilary opined.

'No. No, she isn't. She isn't kind. If I wasn't in love with her I would probably dislike Celeste utterly. But there it is. I'm like a fly caught up in a web.'

'You know what they say about the course of true love?' she ventured, thinking to encourage him. 'Judging by the fact that we are here discussing your problems, our parents must have reached a fairly happy conclusion eventually.'

'Miss Solomon!' he said admiringly, and reached impulsively to kiss her on the lips.

'Aha!' came an imperious voice from the doorway. 'That is a very good way of propagating the common cold virus, I believe?'

Verian stood up insolently.

'A most enjoyable one,' he told Raoul de la Rue. 'Perhaps you've forgotten how delightful it is, Monsieur le Docteur.'

Hilary fidgeted uncomfortably as the door closed on her visitor. The doctor's eyes were at once hot and cold as they regarded her. He took her temperature and listened to her chest in silence.

'Very good,' he concluded. 'I think we have nipped that little lot in the bud. You may get up tomorrow and be careful. A little chat with your patient, a little sunbathing, no exertion.'

'Thank you, Doctor. I appreciate your concern, but I'm sure I'll be all right.'

'I prefer to be sure for myself, Nurse. You are very keen, you say, on your career, and we both know what that involves.'

He turned towards the door, pocketing his stethoscope.

'Thank you,' she said shyly. 'You have been most attentive. I prefer to pay my own bill, of course.'

He spun round to face her.

'The son almost drowned you and the family will pay. Your British independence does you credit, but you should be the last to be inconvenienced by financial burdens. Is there anything else you wish to say?'

She shook her head somewhat miserably. He took offence every time she opened her mouth.

'He grows on you, this young man?' he suddenly inquired.

'Who?'

'This Verian.'

'Oh, that!' she found herself blushing. 'We're not anything to each other, no matter what you saw. I had just been advising him on his love life. I'm not in the least a part of it.'

'Appearances were somewhat deceptive, then?'

'Of course they were. Verian would much prefer to kiss someone else.'

'And you—?'

She looked him straight in the eye, surprised, and the granite of his lips softened suddenly into an apologetic smile. 'As if it was any of my business,' he shrugged. 'See you some time, then. Heed my good advice, Hill-ary. No exertions.' He smiled again, and her heart performed a somersault in her chest.

He was a complex person, and his moods were fast becoming the barometer of her days. He had just left her feeling happier than she had felt for days because he had softened towards her and smiled.

What would she have done—the alien thought crept in—if it was he who had suddenly swooped and kissed her?

'I think I would have died,' she told herself, 'of excitement and happiness. But he would never do it, not by stealth like a thief in the night. If he wanted to kiss one he would let it be known, and then, when it happened, one could co-operate and make a real job of it. Oh, these are stupid thoughts. It proves I've got far too much time on my hands for my own peace of mind.'

The first of September was hot with a stillness which was somehow oppressive. There was a haze over the sun and a breathlessness as of things about to happen.

They certainly did.

Lady Vesper had just settled down to rest—she had complained of not feeling well—when there was a sudden eruption in the quiet house. Hilary was crossing the wide hall intent on preparing an iced drink for her patient when there were sudden screams of youthful laughter and four girls, pursued by two hefty young men, hurtled over the threshold.

'Say!' one of the young men remarked in sudden admiration, 'this is some place.'

The other one spotted Hilary.

'*Some place!*' he echoed with emphasis. 'This one's gonna be mine.'

The girls were now regarding the young nurse with curiosity tinged with hostility.

'Hello!' said one of them, slinking forward a few yards. She was the tallest of them and had an attractive face and wide-apart pansy eyes and long, untidy yet attractive hair. She was a *gamine* sort of creature with coltish limbs and an impertinent stare. 'I live here. I don't know about you.'

'I expect you're Louisa Vesper. My name is Hilary Hope, and I'm a nurse.'

'Oh, it talks!' one of the other girls yelped. 'It talks quite prettily. *Miss* Louisa to you, my girl, if you're employed here.'

Hilary gave her a brief glance and continued to address the daughter of the house. 'Lady Vesper is resting at the moment. Perhaps you would see to it that your friends keep quiet for an hour or so?'

She went on her way towards the kitchen while the refined din broke out behind her once again.

'Fancy telling you what to do in your own house, Lulu. The cheek of the working classes!'

'I guess she's kinda cute,' an American voice decided.

'You kinda like anything female, Rod. You're sexmad.'

'Give, baby, give! Me? I'm *that* kinda mad.'

There was another shriek of laughter and a scuffle.

Hilary came back across the hall carrying a tray of iced lemonade.

'Allow me to take that?' offered Jason, the other American.

'No thank you, I can manage.'

'She doesn't like us,' one of the girls decided. 'You can tell that.'

'Girls don't like other girls,' added Louisa. 'I simply hate you lot.'

'Oh! That's a nice thing to say when you've dragged us all the way from Juan.'

Hilary entered Lady Vesper's room quietly and set down the tray next to the bed. The woman was lying with pads of eau-de-cologne over her eyelids. Without stirring she asked: 'Did I hear my daughter downstairs?'

'Yes, you did, my lady. There's a party of six of them.'

'Dear me! If she hasn't notified Madame they can't all stay here. Louisa's friends are inclined to be, to say the least, distracting.'

Hilary quite agreed, but said nothing. She had

gathered that the less she saw of Verian's sister and her friends the better. She found a quiet corner of the garden and read her book where she thought she would be safe from discovery by the young invaders. Occasionally she heard a high-pitched laugh or a transatlantic wisecrack, but where they were or what they were doing she neither knew or cared, providing they left her alone.

When it was time for Dr de la Rue's visit she once again changed into uniform and went to rouse Lady Vesper.

'You've had a nice sleep, my lady?'

'Yes, thank you. I feel better for it. Will you ring for Marie? I want to get dressed.'

When her ladyship was attired in a pretty afternoon dress Louisa arrived and embraced her parent affectionately.

'Darling, you do look pretty. Are you feeling better?'

'Much. I have a very good little nurse—'

'We've met,' Louisa dismissed the other sharply. 'She told us to shut up, in her own words.'

Hilary bit her lip and was about to slide out of the room when the doctor arrived.

'Raoul, darling,' Louisa greeted him gladly, and deliberately wound herself around him in a long, purposeful embrace.

Hilary felt a queer stab of pain in her chest and turned her eyes away. Louisa's voice was like silk.

'Raoul, I'm nearly nineteen. Of course I'm grown up. You should know your physiology.'

'You're a little cat, Louisa. All purr or scratch.

Now, you purr. Tomorrow . . . '

'Tomorrow I'll still adore you, Raoul. I love, love, love you!'

'Louisa!' said her mother.

'Shush, darling! Don't be jealous. *You* have Daddy.'

'May I be excused, please?' Hilary asked pointedly.

Nobody heard, apparently, or took any notice, so she let herself out of the room and entered her own. In a funny way she wanted to cry, yet there was really no reason for it.

She couldn't account for her sudden depression.

CHAPTER SEVEN

LOUISA VESPER looked at herself in the long mirror and admired what she saw. She had just risen from her bed and was wearing a striped nightshirt, which, although looking as though it should have been on her brother, had been tailored especially to fit this very modern young lady. She liked her own slenderness, her lack of feminine contours. She had been compared with the models who occupied the pages of *Vogue* and *Harpers*, and the comparison did not offend her in the least. She could wear anything and look svelte, and although she practically lived in jeans and ski-pants, she liked to think that, when there was an occasion for dressing up, her lumpier friends envied her greyhound elegance, which was so *à la mode* at the moment now that chiffon-skirted creations were definitely out, along with the dances which complemented them.

She took a shower and dressed in a blouse and shorts; she was intending playing tennis with one of the Americans this morning on the château's own court.

Verian didn't play much tennis, and she was annoyed that he hadn't told the gardeners to keep the turf cut and rolled. She had quickly set them to work on it, but there were bound to be lumpy bits after a few months' neglect.

The three girl friends who were staying in the

house were going into Aurillac with the other American. She was glad. She was getting a little tired of Chrystabel, Sara and Fanny and *Fun*. They always had fun together, but one grew tired of that as of anything else of which one had had a surfeit.

They had picked up the two American students in Juan les Pins, while they had been staying with Sara's parents, the Honourable Marcus and Mrs Willesdon, who had a very nice villa at the famous resort. It was *au fait* to pick up Americans with her set at the moment. They had none of the inhibitions of Britons and were much more fun. Rod and Jason, who were 'doing' Europe during their long vacation, had been promised an invitation to Verian's coming-of-age celebrations in return for bringing the three girls and their luggage to the château from Juan. Having fallen in with British aristocracy so easily, the two Americans intended extracting the last drop of enjoyment from such a situation.

Louisa was also feeling pleased with herself this morning on another account, one she was not yet prepared to confide in anyone else. She had discovered, somewhat to her consternation, that she was still in love with Raoul de la Rue. Last year, when she was still quite young, she had developed a grand passion for the doctor, then new to her family. And she had experienced several violent love affairs, each of which had endured but a short, turbulent season, she had naturally expected this, too, to pass into the realms of the ridiculous. What with a prolonged winter sports holiday and finishing school, with trips to famous fashion salons and picture galleries, she

hadn't really given much thought to her latest be-
loved and felt confident that she had outgrown this
passion as she had others. Yesterday, however, her
heart had leapt to see Raoul arrive to see her mother,
and her own greeting of him, that swift caress of her
young body against his, had aroused her to a fever
pitch of physical excitement. He was still the most
wonderful man she had ever seen, making everybody
else appear juvenile and rather tiresome. Now that
her affections had stood the test of time she was
confident that this great love affair must last for ever,
whether it reached a normal climax or not. It was now
up to her to make Raoul reciprocate and fall in love
with her. She didn't anticipate too much difficulty,
being assured of her powers of attraction and having
learned a good deal on the subject of human relationships during the past year at school.

She knew there had been a girl in his past, an
erudite sort of creature, about his own age, who had
studied medicine with him at the Sorbonne. She had
been killed in an accident on the Metro and it was
said he had never got over it. Well, it was obvious
that much virtue was retained in Yvonne's memory
because of her decease. She would have been quite
old by now, for one thing—about thirty, and everyone knew that women were past their prettiest at
twenty-five. It was up to her, Louisa, to show Raoul
how truly desirable the very young female could be.
They may not have either experience or maturity,
but they had everything else, plus the assurance that
both these commodities would come with time.

'He's almost twice my age,' the girl pondered with

a deep satisfaction as she sought her tennis racquet with a view to having a knock-up on her own, 'which is just perfect.'

Of course the marriage would have to be delayed for a year, for she was due to enjoy a season in London, like the rest of her friends. An aunt already had the arrangements in hand, as Mummy was practically an invalid, and she kept writing to her niece and telling her to make a note that so-and-so's ball was on April eighteenth and somebody else's house-party on the twenty-sixth, and so forth. There was so much to fit in next year and she would scarcely have a moment to spend with darling Raoul.

They would have a secret engagement, she promised herself, and Raoul would be jealous and mortified at all her carryings on. He would probably fly to London and come and abduct her from one of the said house-parties so that they would have to get married because of the scandal.

Oh, it would be an absolute dream, and she would be a wife while her friends were still inspecting the ranks of pimply youths from whom they were expected to choose their partners for both dancing and life.

'So this is where you are, Lulu!' Verian's voice interrupted her mental wanderings. 'There's a character arrived at the house asking for you. He's a Yankee type.'

'That'll be Jason. Send him out to me, darling brother.'

'Who in heck is Jason? I thought he was off somewhere with his Argo-whatsits.'

'Very humorous. Jason is a friend of mine and we're going to play tennis this morning. What are you doing?'

'Nothing, unfortunately. I shall find my idle hands some mischief to do, no doubt. May I umpire for you and the Yank?'

'If you must, darling. You can't do us any mischief because we aren't like that. Jason really plays tennis. He's fierce.'

'Then you umpire and I'll play.'

'Don't be tiresome.' He could beat you with one arm behind his back, wearing a blindfold. Even I can whack you hollow. Where's Celeste? I thought you told me over the phone that that affair was apparently still on.'

'So it was; is, maybe. Time will tell.'

They regarded one another candidly.

'I'm in love,' Louisa said suddenly. 'Isn't it wonderful?'

'You must be in the first stages,' Verian told her grimly. 'It's not so hot later on. You'll find out. Ah, here comes your Yankee.'

'Hi!' Jason greeted happily, leaping over the net and coming to plant a kiss firmly on Louisa's cheek. It was aimed at her lips, but she turned her head sharply, thinking of Raoul and how he would want her to keep her lips for him. 'Hiya, honey!'

'Hiya!' she replied, and turning to her brother, asked: 'Well? Are you staying or going?'

'Going.' He smiled a nasty cynical smile. 'I'm sure you two want to be alone.'

'You betcha,' Jason agreed promptly.

'That's what I like about Americans,' Verian pondered, as he wandered back to the house. 'They're always so shy and retiring.'

Hilary met Dr de la Rue as she was strolling through the village later that morning. He was walking and appeared in good spirits.

'Good morning, Hill-ary! My mother asks if you would come to English tea with her this afternoon?'

'That's very kind of Madame de la Rue,' Hilary responded, feeling at a loss. 'I shall be delighted to come if Lady Vesper can spare me.'

'Of course she will spare you. You are not her shadow. But I will arrange all that. I will send André for you at three o'clock. He is the local cab-driver.'

Hilary smiled and he went on his way, a lithe, athletic, broad-shouldered figure she found herself gazing after in a kind of enraptured dream, so that when he turned his head and saw her she flushed in embarrassment and almost forgot to answer his hand in salute with a twinkle of her own fingers.

After lunch she looked through her dresses and took one down to the kitchen to run the iron over it. Louisa was already there, baking a cake, surprisingly enough. Hilary hadn't imagined her being in the least domesticated.

'Simnel cake,' she explained airily, 'for my sweet Raoul. Don't you think he's a poppet, Nurse?'

'I think Dr de la Rue is very nice.'

'You may call me Louise, you know. Chrys was only ragging when she told you to address me as *Miss* Louisa.'

'I realise that. You do like your little jokes.'

'No, honestly, they're much younger than I am. Mentally, that is. I feel quite old at times, and I simply adore mature men. Do you?'

'I think that would depend on the man, in my case. Some of them are adorable and others the reverse.'

'Then how do you class Raoul?'

Hilary covered her confusion with a laugh.

'We're not coming down to personalities, are we? If *I* said he was adorable you might not enjoy it.'

Louisa popped the Simnel cake into the oven with a sigh of triumph. 'That will be ready when he comes to tea and surprise him,' she announced.

For the first time Hilary wondered if she was to have tea with Madame de la Rue *tête-à-tête*. Her son had not stated that he would be there. In case Louisa was heading for a disappointment she thought she had better mention the invitation without more ado.

'Oh, she's sweet,' Louisa volunteered. 'She loves her little tea-parties and all the gossip from home. She doesn't visit England nowadays. Of course they haven't much money, you know. They're an awfully old French family, proud and well-loved locally. Raoul is really the Squire hereabouts. People think Daddy is, but that's not true. We may have the biggest house, but that's all there is to it.'

Hilary went back upstairs to change.

Promptly at three o'clock an old sit-up-and-beg type taxi arrived to transport her to the de la Rue *maison* and she climbed into the back wearing a red and white dress with a scarf to match.

She hoped she looked nice and when the taxi

rattled up to an old red-brick house tucked into a copse of poplars the first person she saw was Raoul, waiting to help her to alight. There was a slightly stunned expression on his face and his hand held hers no longer than it took for her to reach terra-firma.

'My home,' he indicated the cosy-looking house.

'It's very attractive.'

She was more aware of him than she had ever been as they entered the dark, cool hall, beautifully polished and furnished with antique mahogany tables and a couple of tapestries.

'Maman will see you in here.' He led her into a room which opened on to a terrace overlooking a sloping meadow through which a stream ran in silvery cascades. An elderly lady sat in a high-backed chair awaiting her visitor. Her eyes were as piercing a blue as her son's were grey. There was a warmth of personality and welcome emanating from her, and Hilary took to her immediately. She clasped the outstretched hand and felt it examining her own, finger by finger, bone by bone.

It was then Hilary looked up again into the very blue eyes. She was aware, then, that they rarely blinked, that they looked through rather than at her, or was it that they didn't look anywhere at all, that Madame de la Rue was blind?

Hilary glanced at her son, who placed a finger warningly on his lips for her to keep silence.

'I like your Nurse Hope, Raoul,' said the older woman happily. 'She is all you say. You can leave us now. We will get on very well together.'

'May I have a word with your son, madame? I

won't keep him a moment.'

She walked with him to the front door.

'I haven't anything to say, really. I am right about your mother being unable to see?'

'Yes. But allow her to surprise you. She likes to believe nobody can tell, and when she starts walking about you will understand why.'

'I'm sorry. I mean about your father and—and this.'

'You have a sympathetic nature, Hill-ary, and a remarkable perception. Now you will understand why I can never go back to Paris.'

'Yes. But there will be other opportunities—for you.'

'Thank you. I will be back to take you home. I am having another baby at the moment. *A bientot.*'

She went back to join her hostess with a warm feeling at her heart, as though she understood Raoul de la Rue better than ever she had imagined she would, and coming here into his private world of home and loved one was a privilege she could not but appreciate from the bottom of her heart.

Madame de la Rue was most gracious, charming and friendly. It seemed to Hilary that her son was very much like her, once you really got to know her. They spoke of many things, London and the English countryside, which Madame thought incomparable, despite the merits of rural France. An elderly maid, obviously devoted to the family brought in a typically English tea at about four-thirty, and they had it in the shade on the terrace overlooking the green meadow.

The tea was served from a silver pot into the finest

113

bone china cups. It was the best cup of tea Hilary had enjoyed since leaving home, and it was obvious that an Englishwoman was behind the ritual despite her handicap.

There were farmhouse scones, thick with butter, home-made wheaten bread with cheese and white bread with strawberry jam, and then cakes, both large and small in mouth-watering variety.

Hilary discovered how hungry she could be when the fare was so delicious. Catering at the château was not of the best and one was inclined to live on soups and fruit, ignoring the main course altogether.

It was after the meal, while they were both chattering happily, that Madame said suddenly: 'You *have* guessed, haven't you?'

Hilary knew exactly what she meant and didn't waver.

'I'm a nurse, you see, Madame. I expect I've been trained to be so observant that I notice more readily than others would have done. But no one can tell by your eyes, which are really lovely, or your movements. You had me shattered the way you poured the tea without spilling a drop.'

'Fourteen years' experience, my dear,' the woman said, obviously pleased by the other's amazement. 'Whenever we have a few breakages, and what household doesn't, I sometimes disgrace myself until I get used to the new china. But I refuse to hand the job over to anyone else. I must learn. It keeps me on my toes.'

'You're certainly that, madame,' Hilary said sincerely.

'You're too kind to ask what happened, aren't you, dear?' the older woman said, after a brief pause, as though reading Hilary's thoughts, which was quite uncanny. 'I don't mind in the least talking about it if you want to hear. My husband used to breed horses in these very pastures; fine, noble creatures used at one time in the army and nowadays for police work. They had to be trained in *haute école*, dressage, all that sort of thing. I had learned to ride after I was first married and so I undertook to help with this training. I loved horses almost as much as my dear Philippe did, and Raoul had to be driven away from the stables so that he could attend school. I was still riding when I was fifty, but one is as old as one feels, and I certainly felt young enough for that. Perhaps my reactions were not so quick, I don't know, but one day I was exercising a beautiful, yet excitable, beast in the lanes round here when a stranger, having lost his way, appeared round a bend in a noisy sports car. Usually there was no motor traffic about, and my horse, fairly new to his schooling, reared and threw me. I was perfectly all right; I said I was, immediately, to put the young man at his ease, but I couldn't see. He caught my horse, took me home, and my husband examined me, then a whole string of doctors and specialists. I was in hospital for some time, feeling like a fraud because I was perfectly well, but many examinations only confounded those who cared for me. Apparently there is no known reason for my blindness. It could have been shock, but for some reason the optic nerve refused to function. I was told I could regain my sight as quickly, but I never have, and now I don't trouble about it. What I minded most, when I returned home from hospital, was the horses. My husband had sold them, every one. For some reason he couldn't bear to carry on that side of his work.'

Hilary put her hand out and squeezed Madame's warmly.

'Thank you for telling me your story. You have been very brave about everything and haven't mentioned the bad things, of which there must have been many. You must have minded not being able to see your husband, your son, your beautiful home . . .'

Tears trembled for a moment in the blue eyes and were wiped away before they could fall.

'Now you mustn't make me feel sorry for myself, Nurse Hope. There are so many compensations. I remember my husband as a handsome, vigorous man, and he was very handsome. I also remember myself with some pride and vanity. Those fourteen years have not affected my visual memories.'

Hilary was silent, and it appeared that once again Madame read her thoughts.

'Of course I would like to see my boy. Fourteen years ago he was a rascal of a schoolboy. Now he must be—'

'Very good-looking and attractive, madame. You must be proud of him.'

'Proud, yes, and anxious, as any mother must be who knows her son imagines she is dependent upon him. I want his happiness. I don't want to stand in the way of that.'

'I think he is happy in his work and he has ambitions which may well be fulfilled right here.'

'His children's home, you mean? Yes. He doesn't often speak of that outside of the family. He must think very highly of you. He needs Government help for that project, but he keeps them aware of his existence. The air hereabouts is particularly good for respiratory diseases, especially in winter, and Raoul hopes to gain Government aid in building a children's sanatorium here. Of course if Yvonne hadn't been killed it would all have been much simpler. She was going to be a doctor, too, and they were planning to set up an establishment together and work as a husband-and-wife team. It was a pity about Yvonne, because he hasn't looked at another woman since. I would be happier if he was married, but he does need someone special; someone who can share his profession with him. Do you understand?'

'So many doctors marry other doctors,' Hilary said, 'so they must have the same need.'

'Or a nurse,' Madame went on musingly. 'A nurse would make Raoul a good wife.'

Hilary felt almost relieved when Dr de la Rue arrived at that moment.

'More tea for your son, Maman,' he ordered jovially. 'I have just delivered Madame le Brun of a daughter. That is number five. Poor old le Brun! He has kept champagne in his cellar all these years awaiting the birth of a son. I don't suppose it will be coming out tonight for *la petite*. But she is a pretty little thing.'

'I seem to remember it was a Frenchman who said, "Thank Heaven for little girls",' Hilary observed,

117

and mother and son laughed appreciatively.

'I must remember to tell that to le Brun,' Raoul decided. He sat down happily awaiting another pot of tea, munching a scone and looking round expansively.

'Have you two had a good gossip?' he wanted to know.

'Of course we have,' Madame answered in like vein. 'Gossip, chat, heart-to-heart, all of it. Hilary and I get along very well. We understand each other.'

'Really?' Raoul glanced mischievously at the guest. 'You and I must gossip some more when she is gone, Maman. You must tell me things. *I* simply don't understand her at all.'

'You surprise me, Dr de la Rue,' Hilary returned. 'I'm a perfectly straightforward person.'

'No young woman cares to be fully understood by a member of the opposite sex. Like an iceberg she shows only an eighth of herself above the surface. You agree, Hill-ary?'

'I must consider your statement very carefully. It seems to me that all eight-eighths of me have been involved in learning my job these past three years, but if there is some of me still under the surface I must know about it myself first.'

She rose and smiled.

'I think I really must go back to the château now. It has been lovely meeting you, madame.'

'And very nice for me to have you. I hope you can come again before you go away. Raoul must arrange it.'

As he led her out to his car he asked: 'How long to

118

stay in France, still?'

'Only two weeks.' She sounded almost regretful in her own ears and realized that she would be genuinely sorry to leave. But was her regret for the château and a way of life she had never known before, for Lady Vesper and her family, or for something or someone else? Perhaps this was all part of the hidden seven-eighths she was just discovering existed.

'Only two more weeks, eh? That can be a long time or a short, depending on what you are doing. Time and relativity, you know?'

'I have a feeling it will fly,' said Hilary.

They were now driving slowly along, very slowly, as if they didn't really want to arrive at the château at all.

'Then why don't you get a job in France?' he asked her. 'The same story. Too few nurses, sadly underpaid, as in England.'

'I have a job waiting for me back home,' she explained. 'And I haven't really a valid reason for staying in France.'

'What about the language?' he urged her. 'The best way to learn is to settle among the people. I may even be able to offer you a job later on. When they build my convalescent home you would make a very good Sister-in-Charge, I think?'

These were only day-dreams, she told herself. If that had been a concrete offer she could think of nothing more attractive than working next to Raoul de la Rue for the rest of her working life.

'Here we are,' she announced as the car drew up to

the fine Italian marble steps of the château. 'Thank you for introducing me to your mother. She is a charming person and extremely courageous. I would like to see her again to say goodbye, if I may?'

'That will be arranged, Nurse.' They were being more formal now. It wasn't as if they had ever really become familiar, but they had both unbent a little, warmed towards each other and then withdrew.

Hilary ran up the steps, not even turning to watch the doctor drive away. She went up to her room and changed into uniform before going next door to see her patient.

There was a certain hostility in Lady Vesper's demeanour which at first expressed itself in a cold silence as Hilary prepared a tray for her massage.

'How are you, my lady?' the girl ventured at length.

'What do you care? I'm not at all well, if you must know. I'm upset.'

Hilary took her pulse and found it quite lively.

'I think it's a bit much you and Raoul going off together like that. He seems to forget that you *are* my nurse and I expect you to be on hand when I need you, especially when *he* neglects to call on me as well.'

'He hasn't been in, as usual?'

'You know very well he hasn't been near me. I'm most upset and offended. He evidently thinks it's more important to keep you entertained than attend to his patients.'

At last Hilary responded, massaging patiently the while. 'I've scarcely seen Dr de la Rue, Lady Vesper. I had tea with his mother. When he came in, eventually, he was obviously very tired and said he had been attending a confinement. I think he has now gone to see a dangerously ill patient whom he has also had to leave until this evening. No doubt he will be along later or will phone to inquire after you.'

There was also Louisa to contend with, a Louisa whose pansy eyes were blazing when she confronted Hilary in the hall.

'Of all the cheek!' she flared. 'You knew I was expecting Raoul to tea, the cake and everything, and you kept him with you. Give some people an inch and they'll take a yard every time!'

Once more Hilary explained that Dr de la Rue had been busy with a patient.

'He wasn't busy when he was coming up the drive. I thought the car had broken down and you were both pedalling it, or something, your heads were so close together.'

The other girls were now crowded in an interested bunch in a nearby doorway and squealed with laughter.

'You were obviously paying us great attention,' Hilary returned coldly. 'I happen to have far more in my head than that which apparently troubles you, Louisa. Dr de la Rue and I were discussing the nursing situation in France, and if you've put your cake in an airtight tin it should have improved by tomorrow.'

She went off without more ado, leaving Louisa gazing after her with narrowed eyes. Now her friends were laughing at *her*, and this displeased the daughter of the house more than a little.

CHAPTER EIGHT

HILARY was conscious of a feeling of disorganisation during the next few days. She did not intend to offend Lady Vesper by leaving her alone for long again, for although her employer had insisted she must feel herself to be free to go about as she wished, and had encouraged her to accompany Verian whither he might feel disposed to go, she apparently did not feel quite so hospitable regarding arrangements made between her nurse and her doctor, being fully prepared to imagine offences where none were intended.

So Hilary determined to stay fairly close to the house from now on, and this was not made pleasant for her because Louisa and her friends were determined to extract a certain amount of malicious pleasure from the presence of the young stranger in their midst.

'I'll bet as a nurse you meet up with lots of smashing doctors, like Raoul, all the time?' Fanny Herring accosted her one day.

'I meet many doctors, yes,' Hilary agreed.

'Do you have affairs with any of them?'

'Of course not. That sort of thing happens only in books.'

'But you have to let your hair down sometimes or you'd become frustrated, dear. Verian tells me you're quite a girl.'

Wondering exactly what Verian had said, Hilary found herself colouring up.

'There, you see, Lulu?' Fanny said triumphantly. 'She practically admits that she and Verian have been carrying on. All that butter-wouldn't-melt-in-my-mouth business is just an act.'

Hilary rounded on her tormenter.

'It wouldn't be any use saying there's absolutely nothing between Verian and me, because that's what you want to think and it appears to afford you a pathetic satisfaction. I'm not an innocent child, but neither have I a one-track mind like you people. I think a hard day's work would kill you, and it seems to me particularly pathetic that you spend so much time thinking about love and romance without having the vaguest idea what life is all about. Now, please leave me alone to get on with my job. You bore me.'

She turned away, and almost bumped into Verian in her annoyance and irritation.

'Here!' he seized her firmly as she would have gone on her way. 'Where are you going with such a darkling brow? Have these characters been annoying you?'

'She rattles so easily,' opined Sara Willesdon with satisfaction.

'Guilty conscience,' Louisa said darkly.

'I'll bump all their heads together if you like,' Verian offered.

'Don't bother,' Hilary told him. 'I wouldn't like you to damage them, otherwise they might be my patients, and that I couldn't bear.'

He grimaced at his sister and her friends and went off after Hilary, taking her arm.

'You shouldn't take any notice of them; they're kids, really.'

'Kids who play with dynamite,' she responded. 'Absolutely careless of other people's feelings.'

'I need a sympathetic companion,' said Verian. 'How about it?'

'That would be playing right into the witches' hands,' Hilary told him. 'I've already been accused of carrying on with you.'

'*And* Raoul de la Rue,' Verian informed her. 'Lulu says you've got an acquisitive eye on him.'

Hilary didn't know where to look in her temporary confusion.

'What a household!' she complained angrily. 'I should hate to really fall in love here, with gimlet eyes upon my every move.'

Verian looked at her speculatively.

'You've changed,' he decided. 'Once you were calm waters, good to be with; now you're a turbulent little stream.'

She pondered his words as she took a brief rest in her room, so as to be within earshot of Lady Vesper. She supposed she had changed in these few weeks, and it was stupid, of course, to allow herself to be affected by Louisa and her friends. Her reaction to their remarks was just what they wanted and enjoyed. She had allowed them to see that she was extremely touchy on a subject they discussed very frankly one with the other. Only someone who was secretly in love could be so shy of having that secret made public. If the house-guests were anything of psychologists they would know what it was she was so eager to hide in a blaze of contemptuous anger, and then they wouldn't rest until they discovered who it was who affected her judgment and her temper so.

She was not at all worried about their insinuations regarding herself and Verian, and no doubt he was used to his sister's curiosity regarding his youthful entanglements, but the thought of being hunted down by four determined Dianas, in search of sport, she found disturbing, to say the least.

'I mustn't let them rattle me again,' she asserted. 'They can't help being what they are, and it was I who made it into a class war by my attack upon them. It shan't happen again.'

She had now admitted to herself what had really been painfully obvious for some time. She was in love with Raoul de la Rue. She didn't think for one moment that he reciprocated her affection, but his talk of her staying on in France to continue nursing was his way of selling his country to her, and also he possibly approved his mother's judgment that she was a nice girl and felt friendly towards her.

'Oh, dear! I thought being in love would be a wonderful experience,' she half groaned. 'It's going to be awful.'

Verian had requested that she drive into Aurillac with him after tea, and so, as soon as Lady Vesper was stirring, she asked permission to make this expedition.

'With Verian?' her ladyship asked. 'Of course you

125

may, my dear girl. You're very good for him. I've said so before.'

'Actually I would like to buy him a birthday present,' Hilary said quickly. 'Have you any suggestions?'

But the mother wasn't really any help. She told Hilary, instead, what the family was buying him for his coming-of-age, and gently implied that after a new Italian sports model car and a solid gold cigarette case and lighter, not to mention diamond cuff-links from a grandparent and the key to a summer cottage in Cornwall, there wasn't really much left to offer which was worth the buying.

Nevertheless, Hilary still took her purse with her on the trip, on the principle that a child with all the toys one could imagine in his playbox will still arbitrarily find more pleasure in banging the lid of a biscuit tin on occasions.

There must be something she could afford to buy which would bring some pleasure to poor, spoilt Verian. He insisted on unloading his unhappy heart to Hilary as they drove along in the M.G.

'It's practically all over between Celeste and me, you know,' he told her. 'She keeps telling me to give her time, and the more time I give her the more I'm sure she's seeing somebody else. I still think she's the most wonderful girl in the world, but I'm also admitting to myself that she's not for me. Mama will be delighted, of course. They say one gets over these things. How long, do you suppose?'

'Oh, I don't know.' Hilary felt a sense of fellowship with Verian. 'As a nurse I do know that the

126

human body is capable of overcoming the most terrible physical afflictions. People are literally dying one day, and sitting up getting their teas, figuratively speaking, the next. I expect the emotions are just as resilient.'

In Aurillac, while Verian was buying himself some shirts, Hilary found a bookshop with quite a good selection of books in English. She was quite excited when she discovered the very gift for a young man. It was twenty-one tales of modern-age heroism and was beautifully bound in dark blue and gold. She had it gift-wrapped and was just emerging from the shop when Verian hailed her.

'What have you been up to?' he teased. 'Buying something naughty and French?'

She was glad that he could joke after having accepted Celeste's defection. She hadn't thought it a very good match herself, and Verian would probably fall in love with his new car and give himself a respite from the affairs of the heart.

When they reached St Jude, however, and he saw Celeste walking down the main street in the direction of her home, he hastily asked Hilary if she would mind walking back to the château without him.

'Of course not,' she smiled.

It would take time, she supposed, before he stopped asking for snubs from the lady who preferred not to be his love.

She ran into Michael Smith as she was approaching the château.

'Well, hello!' he greeted. 'I've just seen—' he stopped speaking and coughed instead. 'I heard you'd been ill,' he said. 'I hope you got my flowers?'

Hilary hadn't received any flowers from Michael, but decided against saying so.

'Thank you,' she said. 'They were lovely. I wasn't really ill at all. It was only a cold, but Dr de la Rue made me stay in bed.'

They began to speak of Verian's coming-of-age.

'I've received an invitation,' said Michael. 'Though goodness knows why. Parties aren't much in my line and I can't dance for toffee. But as Celeste's going, I—' he stopped speaking again, and Hilary began to have the dawning of a suspicion in her mind. It was strange that Michael and Celeste should both be in the village at this hour and that Michael should be so embarrassed by his own statements, cutting himself off as though afraid of having said too much.

'Well, it's been nice seeing you,' Hilary said, holding out her hand. 'Thanks again for the flowers.'

Michael and Celeste, now, she pondered as she walked up the long drive to the château. That young lady certainly was having an eventful love-life and could apparently pick up and discard lovers with consummate ease.

There was a large boom shaking the château when Hilary arrived, and she later discovered that it was Sir William, who, having arrived unexpectedly early, was retailing the last year's adventures for his wife's benefit. He had also brought with him two Rhodesian ridgeback puppies, which were irritating Madame Durand by making puddles all over the expensive carpets throughout the château. These were finally removed to regions behind the house while Monsieur Durand was detailed to build a wire enclosure for the puppies.

'William, you really are very naughty,' said his wife fretfully at last. 'You know the Durands hate pets, and I can't take the creatures to England because of the quarantine restrictions. You must take them back to—to Rhodesia, or wherever they came from.'

'Over my dead body,' Louisa contributed. 'The Durands are servants, Mother, and I happen to like dogs.'

'Very well. You get another couple to run the place after they've left us, my girl.'

Hilary saw familiar signs of weariness on her patient's face. There had been enough excitement for one day.

'Excuse me, sir,' she addressed Sir William. 'May I help your wife to bed now? It's much later than usual.'

'Certainly, my dear.' He appeared to notice her for the first time. 'You're a pretty little thing. You're not really a nurse, are you?'

'Yes, I am, sir, and I'm going to ask you to leave this very minute.'

'Come along, Daddy,' Louisa said proprietorially. 'Raoul is coming in for a drink, to see you. I invited him.' She looked meaningly at Hilary as she spoke, and then drew her father out of the room and shut the door very pointedly after them.

The day before Verian's birthday it was obvious that his celebration was no longer going to be a 'quiet little

129

affair' as he had originally intended. Not only were there Louisa's friends staying in the house, but several young men and women, who had known Verian all their lives, made a beeline for the château from the various places where they had been spending the summer, and were accommodated, at the Vesper's expense, in local *pensions* and inns. Members of the family also arrived, including a grandparent, and were put up in the house itself. Extra staff had been hired from the villages round about and the caterers were coming and going, setting up tables in the great hall for the most fabulous buffet ever imagined.

Besides the considerable English community, several nearby land-owners and their families had been invited, so about eighty or ninety people would eventually be helping to celebrate the coming-of-age.

The tennis court was now continually in demand for those athletically inclined, as was the croquet lawn and the archer's green. Lady Vesper had been practically sealed into her private suite, and only members of her family were allowed to invade her privacy. As Dr de la Rue put it: 'So much excitement about and only a little required to undo all our good work.'

Lady Vesper was only restrained from overdoing things by being warned that she might well miss her son's celebration altogether if she didn't take great care. As it was, she retired each night absolutely exhausted, and Hilary was continually taking her pulse and being scolded for 'fussing'. Sir William Vesper wasn't a great help either. Though he adored his wife, and she him, he hadn't any great understanding or tolerance of human weakness. He was like a great boisterous animal, and so energetic and fidgety whenever he was with his lady that he invariably left her feeling tired and drained.

'You're very soothing, Nurse,' Lady Vesper said gratefully as Hilary settled her for the night before the big day. 'I've only just realised how glad I always am to see you about the place. You will stay near me tomorrow evening, won't you?'

'I will, my lady.'

'You must enjoy yourself, of course. Young people like to dance and have fun. But keep an eye on me from time to time and then I'll feel reassured. I am so frightened of being a bore by having one of my turns.'

'Dr de la Rue will be available, my lady, and I'm sure between us we can look after you. I'll ask him to give you a sedative to keep you calmed down, if you like.'

'Yes, yes. Good girl. I'm feeling drowsy now.'

Hilary stayed with her patient until she was fast asleep and then she rang up the doctor's home to inform him of Lady Vesper's fears. He was not in, so she left a message with his receptionist and then decided to give Verian his present while she could still get near him. On the morrow he would probably be busy receiving his guests and their gifts; he would also be inundated with mail and congratulations.

The house was already in a turmoil. There was a family party playing bridge in the morning-room and Louisa and her friends were listening to records in the conservatory. In the small dining-room an elderly member of the family was holding a laborious conversation with Grandmother Vesper, who was apparently either having trouble with her hearing aid or being mischievous about it. Waves of tobacco smoke wafting in through the open windows told of Sir William and his younger brother collecting the ridgebacks to take them for their evening meal.

Nowhere did Hilary see any sign of Verian, however, and she was concluding that he must be out when she heard a lonely thread of music from the west wing, where he had his room.

She ran lightly up the stairs and tapped on the door, despite a sign which said *Do Not Disturb* in four languages. The door opened a couple of inches and then more as Verian saw who his visitor was.

'Come on in!' he invited, and shut the door and locked it. 'I'm feeling sort of sentimental,' he explained, as she glanced towards the record-player where Tchaikovsky was breaking his heart in an unforgettable passage for strings.

Hilary did not look up at Verian. She had a feeling that he had been crying and that he wouldn't want her to know.

'I mustn't stay,' she said. 'Your mother is rather disturbed this evening. I want to stay near her. I thought I would give you this now.' She handed him the book and turned towards the door. 'All the best for tomorrow and the future, Verian.'

'Just a minute.' He had torn the wrapping from the book and was examining the title. 'Thanks, Hilary. It's very good of you—to remember me. I shall read some of it tonight. I know I—won't sleep much.'

'Excitement, I expect,' she told him, unlocking the door and turning the handle.

She was almost through the door when he said, on a note of urgency: 'Before you go, Hilary, please kiss me.'

She would have refused had he not looked so lonely and desolate standing there with the sobbing violins for a background. Keeping the door open, she turned her face up to his, and his lips descended, at first investigatingly and then harshly so that he almost bit her, and she struggled away from him with a small hurt cry.

'Sorry, Hilary,' he apologised. 'I shouldn't have taken it out on you. You see, I've decided to be a woman-hater.'

'Thanks for telling me,' she said, rubbing her mouth and turning to see Raoul de la Rue regarding her stonily.

'I followed you upstairs, Nurse Hope,' he told her. 'I called to you, but you apparently didn't hear. I thought your message sounded urgent, but—'

She wanted to refer to that kissing scene, which he must have witnessed, but felt she couldn't do so without giving it more importance than it merited.

'Lady Vesper had an attack of nerves,' she explained. 'She's afraid of doing something stupid to-morrow. I thought you would like to know.'

'Yes, indeed. You did right to inform me. Is she sleeping?'

'She was when I left her.'

'We'll look in, shall we? Or perhaps you have other plans . . . ?'

'No.' She coloured, unaccountably. Why had he the power to make her feel so guilty when she was completely innocent?

As Lady Vesper was tossing somewhat restlessly they awoke her and gave her a sedative. Raoul chatted to her until she began to feel drowsy once again while Hilary sat in the background. When he stood up she dutifully arose too, and awaited his instructions.

'Naturally she wants to be in on this business tomorrow, but she should really be kept in bed, preferably in a hospital fifteen miles away', he shrugged. 'I'll call in and see her again in the morning. Verian and his birthday—!' he concluded harshly.

Hilary thought this was being a little unfair.

'Verian has a right to his birthday,' she returned. 'He didn't want a lot of fuss.'

'Really?' he asked her, with one of those long penetrating stares of his. 'But then you know him so much better than I do. He and I have never been on what you may call personal terms. Goodnight, Nurse Hope.'

'Goodnight, sir,' she replied as stiffly, and trembled violently when he had left.

What was wrong when one person had the power of heaven and hell over you? He smiled and you were in paradise, but his frown cast you down into an abyss from which he could pluck you again when he so willed.

'I shall hate to go back home,' she sighed as she

134

called in once again on her reposeful patient. 'But it will be such a relief!'

There was a thunderstorm in the night, and Hilary awoke with such a start that she never recovered or went to sleep again. She lay wondering if Verian was awake, too, as he had promised. There was he about to have wonderful gifts and an inheritance showered upon him, and he was grieving over one girl who didn't love him when there were hundreds who would find him most endearing because of his name and possessions.

She slipped out of bed and, pulling on a robe, went in to look at Lady Vesper, who had scarcely stirred since she finally settled down.

There was a small kitchen adjoining her ladyship's bathroom, and Hilary decided to make herself a warm drink. She was sipping this, seated on the chaise-longue in the big window embrasure, when the dawn broke over the far *massif*. It was such a wonderful sight that she watched, enchanted, as grey flushed to pink, orange and then yellow in a hundred different shades which lit up the land mass below with as many enchanting effects.

Hilary felt as though she had never had the time to stand and stare like this before, or felt an awareness of such beauty and grandeur. It was as if, with her awakening heart, other senses had also been sharpened so that it was like seeing beauty for the first time. So it was she played her old game and exclaimed: 'Oh, darling, isn't the dawn simply wonderful!' Only this time 'darling' had an identity, and she hoped that he was seeing it all, too, even though he would not be thinking of her as he kept vigil.

At six o'clock there was a sudden stirring in the great house, not only of the staff about their cleaning tasks but of visitors too, as though the excitement of the day was proving too much for them. Hilary was about to go and take her bath and a cold shower to rally her after the sleepness night she had endured, when round the corner of the house came Verian, running swiftly in bare feet and still wearing his pyjamas. After him, shrieking, came Louisa and her three girl friends. They were shouting something about giving the birthday boy a ceremonial ducking in the ornamental lake behind the house, and Verian was laughing gaily as he eluded them.

Hilary smiled too. She decided that Verian's grief did not cut so very deeply but that a little lighthearted horseplay could quickly bring him from the Slough of Despond back to normality once again.

Electricians were busily erecting strings of fairylights over the terrace and down the twin marble staircase; trees which grew within reach of electric leads were also gaily illuminated and especial care was being given to two spotlights which would revolve and give a snowflake effect during the evening's dancing in the open air. Gardeners were bringing indoors prize blooms cherished year-long for this occasion, and hauling tubs of exotic shrubs into selected places where the lights would show them to best advantage.

The mailman, who usually came to the château on an old bicycle, was replaced by a dark blue van which ejected three sacks of mail and numerous parcels, with which Verian and the young folk busied themselves in the conservatory for more than an hour, like a pop star and his retinue.

When Hilary remarked to her patient that her son must be popular Lady Vesper told her that in their circle many of the cards would be from people Verian had never seen.

'One has a list of birthdays and one's social secretary will see to all that, if one employs such a person, without the principals being aware of one another's existence.'

'I—see,' said Hilary, who didn't, really. She liked to think that the birthday cards she received were sent with love and in sincerity from their donors. How could one wish someone a happy birthday when one knew nothing about it until one footed the bills for the stationery supplied?

Lady Vesper was feeling quite well today, fortunately, and Hilary had to restrain her from essaying forth and taking a hand in the preparations.

'If you're going to dress up this evening and watch the dancing I think you should rest all day in preparation, Lady Vesper.'

'Rest, rest,' grumbled the other. 'Do I ever do anything else?'

'Your husband is arranging a family luncheon party up here to break the monotony for you. I know it must be tedious always to watch everybody else enjoying the fun. I do understand.'

Lady Vesper's blue eyes were damp and then dry again, all within a minute.

'You *are* a nice child, and I shall miss you when you go. I have brought up my own family to be so independent of me and my disability that I think at times they forget I'm a real person who minds being the way I am and can feel lonely and depressed on occasion. William's fond of me as long as he doesn't have to be with me very much, and I would have thought either Louisa or Verian could have found time to say good morning before now.'

'They're all busy, I expect,' Hilary found excuse for them. 'Entertaining the visitors and so forth.'

'You go along too,' Lady Vesper said, smiling once again for Marie's benefit, who had come to help her to dress. 'You must join in the excitement, then you can tell me what you've seen and done when next you see me. I shall look forward to that.'

Hilary did not particularly wish to mingle with the guests, so she found a quiet corner in the gardens where she could observe without being observed. Thus she witnessed the arrival of Verian's new car and noticed his jaw positively drop when he saw it, so well had the secret been kept from him. The young people were all gathered round it, the young men observing on its finer points and the girls climbing in and all over it. Somebody produced a bottle of champagne and the gift was duly 'christened', only Verian objecting vociferously when the operation dented the bonnet of the car before it had even been driven by its new owner. Next about eight people piled into the vehicle and it roared up and down the drive to the accompaniment of feminine squeals.

Being on the outside, looking in, so to speak,

Hilary could enjoy other people's fun without even wishing to be a part of it. She was observing so as to tell Lady Vesper all that was happening, for nobody else would take the trouble, which was a pity.

Verian's old M.G. was next brought from the garage and put up for auction. His guests apparently hadn't much ready cash, however, and the car was withdrawn when the bidding began to creep up to nearly seventeen pounds, after which the novelty wore off and the company drifted off to entertain themselves in other ways.

There was a lull during the afternoon when the younger members of the house-party piled into several cars and went off to invade the nearest neighbour who boasted a swimming pool; the older people all took advantage of the siesta hour, naturally.

Hilary had amused her patient by telling her about Verian's reception of his new car and the ceremonial involved.

'He's a really good boy,' said his mother. 'Or is he a man now? I suppose they are men at twenty-one, no matter how we parents think of them. Now I want him to marry suitably and present me with grand-children. I'm so glad he got over that unfortunate friendship with the Beldame girl. I did my utmost to discourage her, but Louisa tells me she has accepted an invitation to come to the dance tonight. I don't suppose you know whether they've been seeing much of one another, Verian and Celeste?'

'No, I don't, my lady.'

'Well, he certainly hasn't mentioned her to me, and he knows very well how I feel about her.'

Hilary wrote letters in the afternoon while the house was quiet. She was now discussing her homecoming and feeling as though she had been away from everything for years rather than a little over five weeks.

Dr de la Rue called earlier than usual and remarked that Nurse Hope looked as though she hadn't been sleeping.

'Yes, today *she* looks like the invalid,' agreed Lady Vesper.

'I'm perfectly all right,' said Hilary. 'I normally sleep like a top, but there was an atmosphere about last night. One can't have a coming-of-age in the house without being affected by it.'

'You will be at the dance?' inquired Raoul.

Hilary glanced at her patient.

'I shall be with Lady Vesper,' she replied.

'Rubbish!' said that lady. 'I was feeling foolish and sorry for myself yesterday. Today I'm well, and you shall dance your shoes off, my dear, like all the other young people. You have a dress? If not Louisa shall lend you one of hers.'

'I have a dress, my lady, thank you. But I would really prefer to watch the others.'

'Then you will be like Cinderella, and I wouldn't like that. It's quite sufficient that I have to be content with looking on without you losing your opportunities deliberately. You're a pretty thing, and I'm sure our young guests will not neglect you. Verian shall dance with you and so will Raoul.'

'I shall be delighted,' he bowed gallantly, and Hilary blushed in embarrassment. She didn't want

140

anybody to dance with her because they had been commanded to by Lady Vesper. Nevertheless she wouldn't be able to resist allowing Raoul to take her in his arms before they parted for ever.

After tea there was a great deal of activity in the great house. The guests were in their suites being attended by an army of manicurists and hairdressers and couturiers from the nearest city of Lyons. Detectives arrived to keep an eye on the guests' jewels and watch out for gatecrashers. The electricians were trying out the lights and a dance band arrived and tested their instruments and amplifiers. During a break in proceedings a small party of the villagers were to perform a couple of traditional dances in full costume, and a Spanish dancing act had been hired to complete the cabaret.

It was the type of lavish affair that would afterwards be reported in *The Tatler*. There were people with press cards stuck in their hats already taking photographs of the château from various vantage points.

Hilary considered she would be sufficiently dressed up in a full length green silk dress she had brought with her but not yet worn. With it she decided to wear a pale green stole, and approved her appearance though she was really only dressing up at all for the benefit of one pair of eyes. Fortunately she had the kind of hair that required no professional attention. She had washed and set it the previous day and its soft dark folds curled softly over her shoulders. She used a little eye-shadow and coral lipstick; both her eyebrows and lashes were dark enough to need no aids; and feeling she was dressed sufficiently to merit the occasion without stealing the limelight from any of the principals, she went in to see Lady Vesper and to help where she could.

'You look very sweet,' her ladyship conceded from under a hairdryer. '*Ici, Marie. Ici, vite!*'

The elderly servant came at a trot and Lady Vesper instructed her to bring a box from the dressing-table.

'Nurse Hope, come and see my jewels.'

Hilary gasped when she saw the store of pendants, necklaces, bracelets and rings with precious stones winking wickedly from all over the place.

'Lady Vesper, how gorgeous!'

'Yes, they are nice, aren't they? And very valuable, of course. William withdrew them from the bank this morning. What shall I wear for the occasion?'

'Which dress are you having?'

Lady Vesper indicated a creation by Dior that was covered with a plastic dust-sheet. A seamstress whisked the cover away, and Hilary gasped as she saw the rich blue brocade of the dress which would suit her ladyship's colouring to perfection.

'These amethysts, Lady Vesper. They match perfectly.'

'You funny little thing! These aren't at all valuable, just worth a hundred pounds or so. I thought my diamonds. . . ?'

Hilary smiled.

'As you wish, my lady, of course. I thought the colour was so perfect with the dress.'

All at once it became a decision of great moment. Louisa came into the room wearing a dressing-gown and her opinion was sought.

'Nurse thinks the amethysts match my dress, and I must say that I'm very fond of them, they compliment my eyes; but my diamonds are so much more impressive. What do you think?'

'Wear your diamonds, of course, Mummy.'

The diamond necklace and earrings were tried on, Lady Vesper leaning this way and that as she looked at the effect in a mirror.

'Oh, I don't know. I'll try again when I have my dress on. I think diamonds are awfully cold, don't you? They have no soul, somehow, only a hard, bright ruthlessness. Imagine me waxing poetical like that! Don't you think Nurse looks pretty, Louisa?'

'Very pretty,' Louisa agreed after a cursory glance at Hilary. 'Well, I must go and get togged up now, I suppose.'

When Lady Vesper was dressed she decided to wear the set of amethysts after all. Hilary fastened the necklace for her and remarked that the catch was faulty.

'I think it's all right now,' she decided. 'And you do look lovely, Lady Vesper.'

'Thank you, my dear. I'm quite pleased with the effect myself. If you're so fond of this necklace I'll have it copied for a present when you leave. Would you like that?'

'Oh, but I don't expect—'

'Well, we'll see. We'll see.'

Out on the terrace the band struck up a waltz and Hilary felt a sudden thrill of excitement tingle through her limbs.

'Run along dear, and enjoy yourself. I'll be along later when my husband comes for me.'

Hilary needed no second bidding. She was young and there was music and the night was suddenly filled with promise.

CHAPTER NINE

THE men were in full evening dress with conventional white ties, and most of the ladies arrived in long gowns with expensive fur wraps, their necks, ears and hands glittering with jewels. Verian's earlier assertion that there would probably be a small family gathering to mark the occasion of his coming-of-age was an understatement, to say the least.

The affair was lavish to the nth degree, and could not have been more spectacular had it been arranged by Metro-Goldwyn-Mayer for one of their million-pound epics.

Louisa and her friends were hoping for at least some dances to suit the younger age group, but they had all learned to waltz and foxtrot at school dances and were intent upon enjoying themselves whatever happened.

The two Americans, who had hung around the area all this time with the party in mind, were now here, there and everywhere in their hired clothes, somehow managing to look extremely transatlantic.

One of these, the one called Rod, seized Hilary for a quickstep, much to the annoyance of Chrystabel Pryce-Jones, who had adopted him as her particular minion.

Hilary didn't much want to dance every dance. She was quite happy watching the arrivals mounting the staircase and being received by Verian and his parents. Lady Vesper looked like a queen and was sitting on an antique French chair, with high back and scrolled, gilded arms, which looked like a throne and heightened the illusion of royalty.

Raoul was late; it was half past ten before he made his appearance. Hilary had despaired of his coming and was standing near Lady Vesper's new point of vantage by one of the open french windows leading into the magnificent Watteau Room of the château, where the older members of the company were accommodated to watch events, or play cards, as they felt inclined.

The caterers were now spreading the *paté de fois gras* on small crackers continuously, and replenishing the plates of chicken and smoked salmon as they were emptied. There was conviviality around the bar, which had been set up in the hall, and the champagne and cognac were flowing like water.

Hilary kept in the background while Raoul paid his respects to Lady Vesper, complimenting her on her appearance and the magnificence of the occasion.

'St Jude will talk about this for years to come,' he told her.

Hilary sank still further into the folds of the blue velvet curtain as he glanced about him, looking somehow so much more distinguished than any of the other males with his good, yet spare, figure and black, well brushed hair.

He sauntered on to the terrace, and Louisa immediately threaded her arm through his and drew him into the dancing. He danced well, too, Hilary decided, feeling suddenly extremely shy of him and envying the daughter of the house her self-assurance in her relationships with attractive men.

She had come forward a little from the sheltering curtain and jumped as a pair of hands covered her eyes from behind.

'Peek-a-boo!' came Verian's voice. 'What are you doing hiding those twinkling toes behind the horticulture, my dear girl? You look good enough to eat, and as there appears to be a famine in the land, according to those hordes around the buffet, I should watch out if I were you. *Allez! Jouez!*' he commanded her.

She turned to him with a smile, offering her hand.

'Happy birthday, Verian! There hasn't been a chance for me to say it all day.'

'Thanks. No, things have been a bit hectic, haven't they? I must say the family have taken some trouble. If organising this sort of do is what Lulu learns at that school of hers, then one mustn't begrudge the fees. Do you see anybody we know out yonder?'

Raoul was still dancing with Louisa, who was chattering fifty to the dozen and looking very pretty and animated. Michael Smith danced past clumsily with Celeste in his arms, and Celeste was looking at him as though she floated on a cloud.

'One or two,' Hilary said slowly. She heard Verian gulp painfully.

'Do you know,' he said, forcing a cheerful tone, 'that book you gave me, *Twenty-one tales of Heroism*, gave me quite a lift. I was reading it into the wee sma' hours, simply couldn't put it down. Do you think I could ever be a hero?'

'I suppose so,' Hilary assured him. 'Heroism needs the right occasion and a naturally nervous disposition, I should think. There must be something to overcome in oneself before an act becomes courageous. But don't jump in the lake to rescue anyone tonight. You look too nice.'

'I like the way you skip from the profound to the practical, young woman. Come on and let's do this jig together.'

'This jig' was a quickstep, and Verian was quite a good dancer. Hilary enjoyed keeping up with his fancy footwork and noticed Lady Vesper approvingly following their progress through her lorgnette. Though they hadn't realised the fact, the dance was an 'all change' affair, and suddenly the M.C. roared out through his microphone: 'Ladies and gentlemen, please change your partners now!' He repeated this in French while the rhythm altered to a waltz, and Hilary found herself momentarily deserted in the middle of the terrace and re-enfolded in Raoul's arms. She was somehow unsurprised and quiescent. It had to happen some time, and now it had, and it was right and proper that her head should be resting just above this one man's heart.

Louisa's voice came querulously. 'Raoul, you cheated! You turned the wrong way. You should have partnered Sara,' but no one took any notice.

The dance ended and Raoul was still by Hilary's side, still with one arm round her.

'I have been looking all over for you,' he said, and

148

her cup of joy almost ran over at that moment.

'I thought you were never coming,' she said impulsively, and it was as though something momentous had happened to make them understand one another so perfectly, so suddenly.

'I have lost a patient this evening,' he explained. 'I almost didn't come. But I came—to see you, Hill-ary.'

She reached for his hand and squeezed it mutely. This must be a dream, a wonderful dream, of course, but she didn't want to wake up, not yet.

'Come,' he said, and his voice sounded peculiar and muffled. They left the lights and the music and sought the comparative privacy of the conservatory, which, having yielded up its treasures for the great occasion, was now practically empty and in darkness. Out of this darkness, which was somehow warm and shot with excitement, came Raoul's troubled voice.

'Hill-ary, I have tried to overcome what may appear to you to be a stupid infatuation, for you have never given me any encouragement to regard you other than as a colleague in our mutual profession, but I must confess that I will burst if I don't tell you that I am hopelessly in love with you and torture myself with longing whenever I see you. Do I shock you? I hate myself if I embarrass you, my dear, dear love.'

Hilary was sure there were bells ringing in the sky. They certainly rang in her ears and she felt peculiarly weightless. Was this how a declaration of love affected everybody, or was it only when the speaker was Raoul and the enchanted one Hilary Hope?

'I'm not embarrassed, Raoul,' she heard her voice

wobble in reply. 'I'm blissfully happy. I've been feeling the same way about you, but you've never given me a hint. If I'd only suspected—!'

'Hill-ary, you mean—?'

She put up her hand and stroked the dark head above her own, and without any further invitation he bent and took her lips, softly as thistledown and as firm as steel, and as they kissed and merged and drew apart and sighed there were bells and heavenly strings sighing in a celestial symphony that drowned all the normal sounds of the night and the artificial music that mere men created for less blessed beings' cavortings.

She pressed to his heart now, hearing its wild, exultant beat, and her own was not exactly quiet in her chest.

'Hill-ary, I can't believe you feel as I do. You must tell me again, in daylight, tomorrow. I am so happy. It can't be true.'

She put her lips to his again for answer, still not believing this for herself, but taking what she could to treasure against the slings and arrows of future outrageous fortune.

Into that tender, fulfilling embrace came a sharp voice.

'Who's that hiding in here?' A light flashed on, and off again as quickly. 'Sorry!' the voice apologised, somewhat insolently. 'You should have used the lock. There's one on the door.'

The enchanted moment ended with the realisation that there were other people in the world, perhaps unfortunately for the lovers.

'That damned Louisa!' Raoul said harshly. 'She's a naughty child.'

'I think she's in love with you, too,' Hilary volunteered.

'And Verian? He kisses you, I believe?'

'You mean last night?'

'I do mean last night, and perhaps all the other times. I am a jealous lover.'

'You needn't be jealous of Verian. Last night I let him kiss me because he was lonely and unhappy. But it wasn't a kiss in the real sense. And last night I didn't know about you.'

'Thank you for that.'

They were sweet things to say and to hear, but Louisa had succeeded in breaking the spell. Raoul seemed nervous and upset.

'I cannot stay here, Hill-ary, when all I want to do is make love to you. We cannot lurk in the dark like this. Tomorrow I tell everybody and we make plans.'

'No, Raoul. Please, not so fast. Let's keep it to ourselves for a few days until we get used to the idea.'

'As you wish, of course, my darling. Now I am making my excuses and returning to my bereaved family. There is an old wife who will need a sedative tonight, I think. They were very much attached, as you and I will be. So goodnight till tomorrow, *chérie*.'

She tried to hold him, tried not to think that anything would sever between them at his leaving, but she was afraid as she had never been afraid in all her life before. Perhaps she had never possessed anything so priceless as Raoul's love before and so had never had to fear the losing of such a prize.

151

CHAPTER TEN

FOR a few moments after Raoul had left her Hilary
stayed on in the dim conservatory collecting her
thoughts. She felt it would be an ordeal to go back
into the world again after that brief retreat into sweet
love's sacred province, which was at once all there
was to living and yet so little of it. She told herself
that what had been could never be taken away, as
though she half expected there would be no normal
conclusion to her love affair. When she asked herself
why there shouldn't be, if they both loved one
another as they had declared, she knew it was because she was thinking of herself in the same terms as
a little girl who daily presses her nose against the
toy-shop window, worshipping the big, corn-
coloured-haired beauty but never believing she will
one day be its possessor. With the doll actually in her
arms her happiness is tinged with confusion and fear
that she will drop her prize or have it stolen; it is no
longer safe in the window for her and all to see. Now
it is in her sole charge, and the responsibility is
terrifying.

But with the fear of loss went the glory and the joy
of possession. Raoul loved her, and though he had
loved before, she knew it was a treasure he did not
lightly scatter around. Perhaps he had fought his
feelings in the beginning, loth to relinquish what had

152

been his Yvonne's province to another. Hilary was touched to think he was allowing her into such a hallowed spot; she would never be jealous of Yvonne or of what she had held of Raoul's affections. The past did not concern her. The present and the future were ample to contemplate.

She knew she must rejoin the hedonistic throng of party-lovers, no matter how dearly she would have loved to shut herself up alone with her thoughts. She was still Lady Vesper's nurse and it was time she looked at her patient.

But, to compose herself, she walked all round the house first, down familiar paths which she knew intimately, even in the dark, for it was a moonless night. Her light shoes made little sound, and she almost bumped into two men who were conversing quietly in French. She decided they must be guests, probably seeking a little privacy for a quiet smoke and talk, for she could clearly see their white shirts against their dark tail-coats. One of them said, in perfect English: 'Pardon me, miss. I hope we didn't scare you.'

'Not at all,' she said, and went on her way, feeling dazzled, as she came into the full glare of the lights once more.

Lady Vesper was still happy, but told Hilary her necklace had slipped off at one point.

'It's the spring which is a bit weak, Lady Vesper. You must remember to have it fixed.'

'Are you enjoying yourself?'

'Enormously, thank you,' the girl said with deep feeling.

Louisa, who was standing near at the time, gave a snort and moved away.

'Louisa has a headache,' Lady Vesper explained. 'It's been a very long day for all of us.'

At midnight Sir William requested silence and made a speech in Verian's honour. Everyone drank a toast and sang, 'For he's a jolly good fellow' and then Verian responded. He had drunk plenty of champagne and was inclined to be over-emotional.

'And now ladies and gentlemen, which includes my dear, dear family, I too have an announcement to make . . . ' he paused and beckoned. From the throng Celeste joined him, looking very glamorous in a green sheath satin dress which went so well with her dark red hair and cat-like eyes. 'You've been celebrating a birthday, now hear of an engagement . . . '

Hearing a little gasp, Hilary looked at Lady Vesper and saw her slumped in her chair. She rushed to her side and felt her pulse. There was scarcely a flutter, and through pallid lips her ladyship breathed: 'Oh, Verian! How could you?'

Verian, of course, had simply been inconsiderate and careless. In announcing Celeste's engagement, he had hesitated just long enough, before coupling it with Michael's name, instead of his own, that he had given his mother the shock of her life. She had not waited for the end of the announcement before collapsing into heart failure.

Hilary remembered the ampoules of coramine in her possession, never yet put to use. Fortunately she was sufficiently well trained to have slipped one of these, and a hypodermic needle, into her evening

154

bag. She made the injection and felt the pulse of her patient begin to rally into life once more. The blueness left the lips and Lady Vesper sighed and looked around her. Hilary, Sir William and a few friends had made a circle around her so that no one else was aware of anything being wrong.

'Would you take her to her room, sir?' Hilary asked Sir William.

He promptly swept up his wife, who weighed little more than seven stone, and carried her up to her suite where Marie, not being one for parties, was dozing in a chair. He helped Hilary to remove Lady Vesper's finery while Louisa was detailed to telephone Dr de la Rue and Marie fluttered round.

'When Raoul comes you'll see that he attends to Mother?' Louisa asked pointedly as she prepared to leave the room.

Hilary didn't answer. She was much too busy.

Fortunately Lady Vesper now knew that she had jumped the gun, so to speak, and her mind was at least at rest on this score.

'I thought they had been carrying on in secret,' she confided to Hilary, 'and that Verian had merely been awaiting this day to cock a snook at me. I disgraced myself, didn't I? I'm so ashamed.'

'I think you've had enough excitement for one day,' Hilary opined. 'And you weren't the only one who thought what you did until Verian called Michael on the scene and completed the announcement.'

'I hope I didn't spoil things for those two young people?'

'No, you didn't. Fortunately I was near and noticed your distress in time. The party is still under way and not many people know what happened. But you're going to stop talking now, and rest. Dr de la Rue should be here soon, and I'm sure he will agree that a good rest will put you to rights again.'

When Raoul came he made no sign that there was anything of a deeper nature between them, and of this Hilary entirely approved. A sick woman was not a vehicle through which secret, amorous intelligence could be passed from one to the other; for the time being she was all that was important to both of them, and Louisa, who had accompanied Raoul to the sick room and was all eyes for tell-tale signs of emotion, was confounded and wondered if her eyes had deceived her when she had switched on the light in the conservatory earlier.

Fortunately Lady Vesper had rallied from her shock better than had been hoped; she was obviously much stronger than of late, and she was given sedatives and settled for what remained of the night, with instructions that she was to rest and keep quiet all the next day, also.

Raoul departed, still closely attended by Louisa, and Hilary hauled the chaise-longue nearer her patient's bed and prepared to spend the night as vigilantly as she could even though all did now appear to be well.

When Lady Vesper awakened, about seven in the morning, the first thing she saw was her nurse investigating the faulty clasp of the amethyst necklace.

'What are you doing, up and dressed, at this unearthly hour after such a late night?' the woman promptly inquired.

'I've been here all night, Lady Vesper, keeping an eye on you. I take it that you're feeling well this morning?'

'I am, my dear, thanks to your prompt action when I was so very naughty at the party. You must run along now, and go to bed. Marie will be along shortly, and she can put these trinkets away for me. I promise not to leave my bed today without permission, so rest content.'

Hilary thankfully went next door to her own room, where she flopped into bed and was asleep in a matter of minutes. She was rudely awakened after a short time, however, by Marie, who beckoned her to come to see Madame immediately.

Thinking her patient had had another bad turn, Hilary pulled on a dressing-gown and presented herself, discarding sleep like a cloak.

Lady Vesper regarded her with those keen blue eyes of hers. It was a few moments before Hilary noticed that Sir William, Verian and Louisa were all gathered in the room and all were regarding her sharply.

'What's wrong?' she asked her, her brow creased in puzzlement.

Louisa interjected: 'What *should* be wrong?' but Verian nudged her into silence.

Lady Vesper said: 'You say you were in my room all night, Nurse?'

'Yes—yes, I was.'

'Were you awake?'

157

'The whole time. I felt drowsy at four o'clock, but I made myself a cup of coffee and roused myself. Why? Has something happened?'

'My jewel-case has gone, complete with contents. Marie says it was still here when she left us last night. With all the commotion I caused it was left here instead of being put in the safe, where it should have been, of course. Leaving a thing like that around is asking for trouble. I wondered if you could offer any explanation, Nurse?'

'No, I'm sorry, I can't.' Hilary felt shocked and shaken, but tried to think when she had last seen the jewel-case. 'I didn't notice the box on the dressing-table when I cleared away last night. I think I would have done if it had been there, but I wasn't really looking for it, of course.'

Lady Vesper again questioned Marie, who burst into tears and expostulated loudly.

'She says it *was* there when she left. I've known Marie a good many years and refuse to think ill of her. You're sure no one came in here last night besides yourself, Nurse?'

'No one,' Hilary said somewhat shortly.

'Well,' Lady Vesper handled her amethyst necklace affectionately, 'I still have this, which you so much admired, at least.'

'Yes,' Louisa said cuttingly. 'And if you had heeded me, instead of Nurse Hope, you would have been wearing your diamonds and still had *them*. I don't know how you could allow anyone to influence you so much, Mother.'

'I think I'd better inform the police,' decided Sir

William. 'Fortunately everything is insured, my dear, but we'd better set the usual wheels in motion.'

'Don't you think we should search everybody in the house first?' Louisa demanded. 'If they're not guilty who's going to object?'

'Do hush, Louisa!' snapped her mother. 'The police will do all that is necessary. You may go now, Nurse Hope, but you will be in your room or near, won't you?'

'I will be available when I'm required, my lady,' Hilary agreed, trying to keep her temper in check, for she felt the family was falling over itself backwards trying not to accuse her openly of having been involved in the disappearance of the jewels.

She couldn't think of going to sleep now, however, and dressed, wondering if she would be expected to carry on with her normal duties while she was suspect number one.

A couple of detectives arrived within the hour, together with the two 'specials' who had been on duty at the dance. They were closeted with the Vesper family for some time before Hilary was summoned to attend. One of the detectives was holding a ring with a large green stone, an emerald, wrapped in a piece of white cotton material.

'Do you know anything about this, Nurse?' he asked Hilary in French.

'No, no, I don't,' she told him, understanding perfectly.

'It was discovered in your room. The maid found it when she was cleaning. It is one of the missing pieces belonging to Lady Vesper.'

CHAPTER ELEVEN

ONCE again the immediate family of Lady Vesper looked expectantly at the young nurse, Louisa giving a decided snort.

'I would like to say,' Lady Vesper said clearly, from her bed, 'that I think we should keep this business among ourselves. We have guests, who would be most upset and embarrassed by all this, and I would prefer not to have them involved in a police matter. I would never live it down. I feel sure this has been a straightforward burglary by outside influences, that somebody entered this room while Nurse was temporarily distracted, and that she has an explanation ready for the presence of my ring in her room. Maybe she borrowed it. It's not terribly valuable and I wouldn't have objected. Perhaps I said she could. I'm a little confused myself.' She looked encouragingly at Hilary, who looked stonily back at her.

'You did not give me permission to "borrow" any of your jewels, Lady Vesper,' she said quietly. 'And I can't account for the ring's presence in my room. Perhaps the rest of the jewels are there, hidden under the mattress?'

Verian said uneasily: 'Steady on, Hilary. Nobody is accusing you.'

'Aren't they?' Hilary asked cynically.

'Yes,' Louisa agreed. 'Aren't they? I mean, if I had spent the night with the jewels and then one of them was discovered in my room, I would think *I* was being accused. It's up to Nurse Hope to clear herself.'

'And while you're waiting for that,' Hilary flashed at her, 'the real thieves are getting further and further away with the valuables. You're all putting too much credence on Marie's word. She is getting old and she sleeps very easily, almost unaware that she does it. When we brought your mother in here last night Marie was startled out of her sleep. Nobody was interested in the jewels at that moment and they could have been gone. Now that I remember, I saw two men round the back of the house just before midnight.'

The senior detective understood English.

'You were round the back of the house yourself, then, near midnight?'

'Yes,' Hilary said levelly. 'I took a walk. I thought it was odd that the guests should be there in the dark when there was so much going on elsewhere.'

'Yet was it not odd for you to be there, mademoiselle?'

'No, I don't think so,' Hilary replied stonily.

'Perhaps you were not alone, mademoiselle?'

Hilary bit her lip vexatiously at the questioning.

'When I saw the two men I was alone. They were looking up at the back of the house.'

'They'll be climbing up the drainpipe next,' Louisa interjected impatiently. 'Let's keep to the facts, for heaven's sake. Don't forget I saw you in the conservatory and you were *not* alone. Why cover up your real activities with a lot of stupid falsehoods?'

'I do not tell lies!' Hilary flashed.

'Were you in the conservatory with someone?' asked Lady Vesper.

Hilary looked hunted. She didn't want to bring Raoul's name into this unpleasant scene.

'Go on!' Louisa encouraged. 'Shame the devil. Who was the recipient of your favours, Nurse Hope? Don't be shy. We're all broadminded here.'

'I don't think the identity of my companion in the conservatory is relevant to this inquiry, unless you do, Louisa. Would you like to name him? I'm sure he would appreciate such lack of taste on your part.'

'Children!' Lady Vesper interjected. Her cheeks were flushed and she was actually enjoying the unexpected excitement of the situation.

'Oh, Mother,' Louisa said rudely. 'Do shut up, darling. You think your nurse is a little white dove, but she could have brought an accomplice in here last night. I saw her in the conservatory, but I didn't recognise her companion. When I put the light on his back was towards me, and as the scene was somewhat embarrassing I switched off pretty quickly. I don't say she's a criminal, but you know what girls will do when they're in love, and I would think she was in love. It looked that way to me.'

'Don't talk such utter rot, Lulu!' Verian suddenly shot the bolt, seeing Hilary's obvious confusion and distress. 'I was the mysterious Mr X in the conservatory with Hilary last night, and she loves me about as much as a sore thumb. I was doing all the necking; I'd had plenty of champers, and she was just being her

162

usual tolerant self and trying to get me back to my guests in one piece. Now accuse *me* of taking Ma's jewels!'

He smiled at his sister, who promptly slapped him across the face in her temper.

'Verian, you fool! You've spoilt everything. You—' tears of frustration gathered in her eyes as she realised she could not, now, introduce Raoul's name into the proceedings without admitting she had lied. She had wanted the information to be dragged out of Hilary, for him to be humiliated when he heard of it. She now hated them both so much that she imagined if their two names were linked in the papers, associated with a scandal such as last night's burglary would prove to be, then there would be a quarrel and an end to the hateful affair. She knew that Raoul hated nothing so much as having his private emotions made public, and now Verian had taken his most powerful weapon clean out of her spoiling hands.

As Verian would have struck his sister back, most ungallantly, Sir William intervened.

'We've called these chaps in,' he nodded in the direction of the detectives, who were observing the scene with professional interest, 'why don't we let them get on with it? Who cares what went on in the wretched conservatory? God knows we've all been young.'

'I agree,' the Superintendent said with a smile. 'Our *moutons* await. Perhaps you may leave us now, mademoiselle?' he suggested to Louisa.

'Very well.' Her brow was thunderous as she turned away to the door.

'And say nothing to anybody else,' Lady Vesper called after her.

'May I go, too?' Verian asked, rubbing his flaming cheek. 'I'll keep mum too, Mum.'

The detective smiled and nodded assent, and Verian winked at Hilary and left, leaving her feeling a burden of gratitude which was tinged with regret that his statement that he had been with her in the conservatory was untrue. If the case ever came to court he would have to retract and make a truthful statement of his night's activities, but, with luck, the burglars would be found and the household not subjected to questioning.

As Louisa had been so eager to drag Raoul's name into the light, so Hilary had been equally eager to keep him out of things. She knew he would hate to be sprung on Lady Vesper as her nurse's admirer until he was ready to make an announcement himself. He would want to propose, be accepted and have a date set for his marriage before he let anyone else into the secret. That was his way, and she knew it as though the mysteries of love had revealed him to her and given her a secret knowledge.

Sir William also left to attend to his guests, some of whom were preparing to leave the château to seek other diversions elsewhere.

Hilary was left with her patient and the detectives, wondering what was to happen next and feeling not a little apprehensive. If the real thieves were never caught would she always be under suspicion of this dreadful thing? Louisa, for one, would be slow to let her go free.

'*Monsieur le Superintendent*,' Lady Vesper spoke clearly, beckoning Hilary to her and putting a thin white hand on the girl's shoulder, 'I want to state here and now that I have every confidence in Nurse Hope. I did think she might have borrowed the ring, but if she says she didn't then I believe her. You must look elsewhere and get on with it.'

'Yes, madame. Is there somewhere we can talk with mademoiselle alone?'

Lady Vesper indicated Hilary's own room, and Hilary went in followed by the detectives, where she sat for a full hour having her fingerprints registered and her statement taken down and checked and re-checked. The policemen were interested in the two men Hilary had seen, for though it had been dark at the time she could give their heights; one had been a little taller than herself, about five foot six, and the taller one had a clipped moustache, and he was the one who spoke English with a heavy French accent.

'You will please not move out of Lady Vesper's suite, mademoiselle, for the present,' the senior detective advised. 'You have been most helpful, but there will be more questions, I'm afraid, and we must know where to find you. Also your evidence might be affected by contact with outsiders. Please keep to our rules voluntarily, and we will have no need to confine you.'

'Confine me, monsieur?' Hilary asked. 'You mean I *am* under suspicion of complicity in this affair?'

'Do not think harshly of us, mademoiselle. We are policemen and must not be sentimental. I am sure all will be well and that explanations will quickly prove

165

you are innocent. But circumstances, you must agree, have not so far been in your favour. One of the missing jewels has been found in your room, by a cleaning woman who did not guess at its value or, had she been dishonest, she might have kept it for herself. Your bedroom window has also been the means of entry and departure for the thieves. Had they your confidence? You would naturally say no. We must, at this stage, keep an open mind about such things. Naturally we will study our files and criminal records to see if we can find the two characters you have described. I, as a man and a father would say: 'Fear not, little one, you are as innocent of this crime as the morning,' but as a policemen I say be still, and do as you are told. We will see you again.'

Still feeling stunned by all that had happened, Hilary went back to Lady Vesper.

'I suppose they told you that I'm confined to your suite,' she asked bitterly. 'I already feel like a criminal, and may even begin to think I'm guilty if this goes on much longer.'

'Don't be foolish, my dear. I must confess that at first I thought you might have been guilty—' Hilary looked at her—'of carelessness. You could easily have fallen asleep last night and have been scared to admit it, but I soon saw that you were telling the simple truth and sticking to it, whereas poor old Marie's story has changed at least half a dozen times already. Raoul came while you were in there with the police. I hope you don't mind, but I told him you were out. I didn't want to tell him what had happened. There's no need for anybody else to know unless they fail to find a lead within a reasonable time.'

It was a shock hearing Raoul's name. Somehow Hilary wanted to avoid thinking of him and all they had meant to one another for such a short, sweet time. Then she had intruded a little into Paradise, but now she was in a kind of hell where people had driven her who had attacked and accused her and baited her and left her suspended awaiting events. It was a dreadful time and she could not quite believe she was so involved. In a way she would have liked Raoul to know of her dilemma, to have his love and understanding and strength behind her; but she was also glad he didn't know of her humiliation. Supposing he, too, had wondered for one moment if she could possibly be guilty of complicity in the affair; how could she have survived thereafter? Being in love with someone might well be an uneradicable fact, but affirming the same assurance as to their character, another kettle of fish altogether. Even Mata Hari, rich in her emotional conquests, still left much to be desired as a person.

'Am I still to be your nurse, Lady Vesper?' she asked numbly. 'You don't have to keep me on, you know. Please tell me.'

'My dear, of course you're still my nurse. I have every confidence in you. Didn't I tell the police so?'

'It didn't appear to deter them. They still want me to hold myself for questioning.'

'That's just official jargon. And you must admit to wandering off last night, after all, allowing Verian liberties he simply shouldn't have taken. I'm surprised at you, Nurse.'

Lady Vesper was smiling, but Hilary was not. She didn't care for being indulged youthful weakness with the wrong man.

'Your son wasn't with me in the conservatory, my lady. He saw I was in trouble and stepped in to help me out. And I have no intention of saying who was with me no matter what happens, so if you care to tell that to the police they can make what they like out of it!'

Having hurled this defiance Hilary was relieved when Lady Vesper did not press her for more information.

'There were many attractive young men at the ball,' she decided, 'and you did look very nice. But why is Verian being so helpful all of a sudden? One would imagine he was in the middle of reading a book about heroes.' Hilary gave a wry smile despite her predicament. 'He has always been readily affected by current literary trends. After reading *Jekyll and Hyde* he would be a devil in the morning and an angel by dinner-time.'

Somehow the time dragged on. Hilary had always thought her patient's suite to be extremely large and comfortable, but now the walls hemmed her in and at times she was aware of an overpowering desire to escape and run in the fresh air. She was so attentive of Lady Vesper that she was accused of 'fussing' and at last subsided with a book on a chair near the open windows overlooking the late summer tints of the September scene. She could not settle to read, however, and enviously watched Louisa and her friends boisterously running and playing with the priceless pups on the lawn.

The detectives returned in the early afternoon and once again shut themselves with Hilary in her room. This time they had brought pictures of rogues known to be expert thieves, and when Hilary picked out two who just might have been the men she had seen, the superintendent became quite excited and then put her to another test. She had heard the men speaking together in French, he reminded her. Like England, France was divided up into districts, each district having its own dialect or vocal inflection. He had brought a young detective with him who was a good mimic, and while he recited a line of poetry in various dialects Hilary had to turn her back and signal when she thought she heard one that was familiar from that brief encounter.

It was difficult, of course, for as all English people appear to speak the same English to the foreign ear, so is French simply French to one who has had knowledge of languages in a schoolroom for the best part. But Hilary was more than usually observant, thanks to her job. Three times she signalled, and then the superintendent told her that she had picked out what was the Oxford accent of France.

'Obviously, these men, or one of them, was well educated,' he told her. 'A Raffles, in fact.'

'He spoke such good English I had already concluded as much,' Hilary told him, feeling tired of the whole business. 'You wouldn't expect a country bumpkin to be mixing with this company, would you?'

'Be patient with us a little longer, mademoiselle, we may be getting somewhere. These men you picked out have worked together, which you were not to know. The tall one is a discarded son of an old family, who has gone from bad to terrible, having also been kicked out of the Foreign Legion, and they take practically anybody, as mademoiselle will appreciate. The other is the working member of the partnership. He is what you call *le chat* burglar. He can get in and out of a six-inch drainpipe if necessary. What is it?' he demanded of the man who had been watching the door and now tapped and entered. 'You are wanted on the telephone,' he told Hilary. 'I will wait.'

Hilary wondered who could be phoning her. The call had been put through to Lady Vesper's room and she was conscious that anybody in the house could be listening as she took up the receiver.

'Hill-ary?' came Raoul's unmistakable voice. 'Where were you this morning? What energy after such a night! I overslept.'

'Oh, hello,' she said, aware that Lady Vesper was only three feet away and the detectives had the connecting door open to her room. Probably one of them was recording the conversation in another room, for she fancied she could sense a bated breath on the line. 'Dr de la Rue? Can I help you? Would you like to speak to her ladyship?' There was a pause.

'Hill-ary?' came again in a puzzled tone. 'That *is* you?'

'Yes, this is Nurse Hope.'

'Oh!' came with a laugh of understanding. 'You

are not alone, darling. You like my English "dar-ling?" I have been practising. Well, you listen and I talk to you. You will come to tea this afternoon?'

'Er—no. Sorry, I can't.'

'Why not?' came on a somewhat sharper note.

'It's impossible, Doctor.'

'You mean you are going out with someone else?'

'I'm otherwise engaged. It's quite impossible, Doctor.'

'What the hell do you mean—impossible? Do you love me or don't you?'

Hilary felt a little bit sick, thinking of the eaves-dropper on the line.

'Will that be all, Doctor? I'll carry on with the injections as previously.' She replaced the receiver without more ado, not daring to think of Raoul's expression at the other end of the line.

She was next taken off by the detectives to the local police headquarters to make an official statement and sign it. While she was thus engaged a stormy-browed Raoul arrived at the château for the second time that day.

'Where is Nurse Hope?' he demanded of his patient, automatically taking her pulse and regis-tering that it was much stronger of recent days.

'She is out, my dear Raoul.'

'But she was out this morning also.'

'Why not, dear boy? I don't keep the girl a pris-oner.'

She wondered whether to let the young doctor into the secret of the missing jewels, but decided against it. Having exacted a promise of discretion from

171

everyone else she must not break it herself. She fancied that Raoul was put out about something, but was not sufficiently interested to question him.

He said: 'I'm going back home now, to my mother.'

'Oh yes? How is she?'

'This morning she had a bad fall. Fortunately she broke no limbs, but she is sadly shaken up. There is, however, no holding her. You see, her sight has returned.'

'How splendid! How really splendid! I'm so happy for you.'

'It may not last. We are advised not to hope too much. On the other hand some small obstruction may have been removed by her fall and she may see for the rest of her life. All this may interest Nurse Hope from a professional viewpoint. Perhaps you will tell her?'

'I will indeed, dear boy. Give your mother my regards. You must bring her to see me as soon as she is fit.'

The conversation was forgotten, almost as soon as Raoul's car had sped down the drive, however, and as Sir William came to entertain his wife with a game of Scrabble in French shortly afterwards, and this became quite hilarious, Hilary had been back some time before Lady Vesper recalled that she had been asked to pass on some information to her nurse.

'Raoul was here again. He was somewhat distracted. He said you may be interested to hear that his mother—she was blind, did you know?—had suffered a fall and recovered her sight by the same accident.'

'How wonderful!' Hilary exclaimed, thinking that at least one good thing had happened today. 'I would like to go and congratulate her, see how she is. May I?'

'Well—are you supposed to?'

'Go out, do you mean? They told me to hold myself in readiness as before. Oh, damn! I'm going and that's that. You can tell them where to find me, Lady Vesper.'

But when Hilary was halfway to the main gate an anonymous figure slipped out of the bushes to accost her.

'*Où allez-vous, mademoiselle?*'

She told him, but the policeman informed her that she was breaking her parole and must go back to the house. Monsieur le Docteur, he added, could be reached by *le téléphone*, and that was that, her attempt at defiance was nipped in the bud. After that she found a young policeman posted on the landing outside her room, wearing plain clothes but obviously on duty. She was as much cut off from Raoul and his mother as though she had been removed to gaol and put in the condemned cell. When she did try to contact Raoul by telephone, when Lady Vesper was sleeping, she found Louisa already holding a lengthy conversation and holding the line. Later on there was no reply and the exchange informed her that another doctor was taking Dr de la Rue's calls for the night, so she capitulated to a perverse fate and went to bed.

173

The next day being Sunday, Raoul did not call at the château. He rarely came on the sabbath unless he was summoned, and this day was no exception. The telephone exchange was again passing all calls through to the relieving doctor and it was obvious that if anybody wanted to see Raoul they would have to go to his home to do it. Probably he expected her to do this.

What a mess it all was! If only she could have explained why she couldn't set foot out of the house without a police escort, but this she had promised not to do until the business was cleared up, and she felt bound to honour her promises.

The day dragged miserably by. During the afternoon she was given permission to stroll in the grounds, but the policeman was always quietly in evidence, and when she asked if she could visit a friend he told her, emphatically, that her privilege did not extend this far.

She was glad when Monday morning dawned, a day when something could be done and events put in motion once more. The superintendent visited her to tell her that if the burglars kept to their usual *modus operandi*, as they invariably did, then any day now they would sound out one of their fences to relieve them of their loot, and then she could well be cleared of all complicity and allowed to carry on normally.

'Sir William is offering such a substantial reward for information that no fence could resist,' he told her. 'If they are caught, you too, will receive part of the reward.'

'I'll take nothing,' she said hotly. 'All this has been

humiliating enough without rewards of any kind. The very idea!'

Mail arrived from home, and one letter was from the matron of the hospital where Hilary was expecting to return to work.

' . . . will you please confirm that you can start work as staff nurse on the women's cardiac ward on September 25th, as previously discussed? I would like your answer within a week, so that if you have, in the interim, made other plans I can make alternative arrangements . . . '

Once again Hilary panicked. What could she tell Miss Wattkyn without consulting Raoul first? It was all such a mess. And would the hospital still welcome her if the business of this grand larceny was still not cleared up? It seemed that all her future was in a state of suspension, but life wasn't. Life went on, and so did the good jobs, such as staffing on the cardiac ward of a famous hospital.

She would have to reply to Matron, but did she say yes or no? It all depended on Raoul, and it seemed a long, long time since she had been folded into his arms and heard him whispering impassioned words into her ear.

That day of complete silence between them yesterday was somehow significant. Maybe emotions had cooled and the hardness of the head taken over. Who could tell until they met and saw one another again, without other eyes observing them and other ears listening to their conversation, what would happen and whether they both felt the same about one another with an unkind fate slinging brickbats at their vaunted love?

Could it survive this test of separation and mis-understanding? Hilary doubted it, and betrayed her own name. She had never 'hoped' less in all her life for a happy conclusion to the affair.

CHAPTER TWELVE

OF course they had to meet, Hilary and Raoul, and when they did it was awful.

Who could tell that little more than forty-eight hours had passed since their last impassioned meeting! A stranger came into the room, cold, arrogant and hard, and not once did he seek the young nurse's eyes or the mute appeal for understanding which lay in their haunted depths.

For his own part he had feelings, which he was now hiding as though they were a miser's gold, considering they had been rudely trampled upon by one who had not lived up to his ideals of either sincerity or love.

Hilary had professed a regard for Madame, his mother, and her affliction, but when that affliction had been suddenly, startlingly removed, she had shown not one flicker of interest. She had neither called in person nor sent a message. No, she had been gadding off probably with other young folk nearer to her own age. She must have known that for a woman of his mother's age, the fall itself was a serious thing. But had Hilary shown concern for the bruises, the shock, the possible unseen injuries? Not a jot. It might have been an everyday occurrence for all Hilary had done about it, and yet this was the girl he had hoped to bring to his home as his wife, which was unthinkable.

He didn't doubt but that she had suffered a change of heart towards him; in all fairness he really believed this. But his own way was to be frank about such things, not to suggest it by neglect and innuendo. If Hilary was slinging his love back in his teeth he would have preferred her to say so, and that would have been like a clean, sharp thrust, over and done with; not a nagging doubt which became an abscess of misery with time's passing.

When he returned to his house each day to watch his mother's progress, she was being cared for by an old nurse who often helped him with his cases; he always asked his housekeeper who had called, and when Hilary's name was not mentioned he thought more and more about that odd telephone conversation he had held with her.

He had realised she was not alone, but she could still have conveyed her feelings to him in some way. As it was she might have been a robot on the line; it was as though she didn't want to remember that scene in the conservatory, as though she was embarrassed by it. Well, telephones were the most impersonal of messengers at times like these. He had been glad to have the exchange disconnect him for the weekend. When Hilary called in person it would be different and they could pick up where they had left off in the conservatory.

But Hilary had not come to him.

How he had brooded about it!

Now, today, he fancied he knew the answer. She was young, frightened by all that was involved in marrying him, a strange land, a new way of life. Love was not enough, or she did not know what love really was, as yet. It was clear that her love did not measure up to his, and he had found this out in time, the bitter humiliating way. Well, she need not fear. He would not remind her of a scene she so obviously now regretted. If she had anything to say, let her say it. He would not step over the borderline of strictest propriety. She need not fear him, that he would claim her for a moment's weakness of the flesh.

He was amazingly bright with Lady Vesper, drawing her laughter with observation and anecdote, but Hilary might not have been there save as a prop for the sphygmomanometer when he was using it to take her ladyship's blood pressure.

'And how is your dear mother today?' inquired Lady Vesper.

'Yes, how is she?' Hilary echoed unhappily.

He thought that her unhappiness was for embarrassment over her neglect, and his glance ricocheted from her and back to his patient.

'She is very much better,' he affirmed. 'And the ophthalmic specialist has now been to see her. He thinks she will see as well as ever, with spectacles. She is, of course, nearly twenty years older since losing her sight, and eyes age like anything else.'

'I'm sure you're delighted,' said Lady Vesper, and Hilary, who found her tongue inclined to stillness again echoed:

'Yes, you must be delighted.'

Addressing the room, he said: 'I believe your time is almost up here, Nurse Hope?'

'Well, yes,' said Lady Vesper, again seizing the

initiative as Hilary hesitated. 'I promised Hugo Merlin-Smythe I would return her safe and sound, during this week, some time. But Nurse isn't quite ready to go, are you, dear?'

Her glance warned that quite enough had been said, and Hilary lowered her eyes.

'A—a few more days,' she muttered.

'Well,' Raoul announced clearly, 'I must go and make a few more calls. Does anybody want a lift into the village?'

This time he looked directly at Hilary, and the colour mounted her cheeks.

'No—no, thanks.'

He shrugged. 'Then goodbye!'

Somehow she was at the door ahead of him.

'You—you don't understand,' she whispered.

'Oh, but I think I do. I understand perfectly.'

Her hand reached out to restrain him, but Louisa was coming along the corridor and she allowed it to drop back to her side.

'Goodbye!' he said again, saluted Louisa and ran lightly down the stairs.

It looked, at that moment, like being the shortest love affair on record. It had lasted exactly twenty-five and a half minutes.

Hilary wrote to Miss Wattkyn that she was, indeed, interested in the staff nurse's job offered her, but that she might be delayed in France longer than expected. She didn't say why, but determined to take Sir Hugo into her confidence the moment she returned to England and ask him how the humiliating affair of the burglary might be expected to affect her own future if it was not cleared up.

By the time Friday dawned she had given up all hope of its ever being cleared up, but in the meantime the wheels of the French Department of Criminal Justice were turning inexorably, and when a diamond bracelet turned up in Monte Carlo, which proved to be one of the missing pieces, the villains were apprehended within twenty-four hours, still having much of the loot in their possession, not having been able to find a fence who would take it.

Having been discovered, they were quite ready to tell their story, and laughed at the idea of the young nurse being involved. They had been leaving the house with their haul when Hilary had seen them, and explained that the break-in had been so simple as to be child's play. Only one old woman asleep and the jewel-box there for the taking. Their derision angered the police, naturally, but Hilary was relieved to be free of surveillance. She was now anxious to get back home and pick up the threads of her hospital work if that was what her life was to mean from now on.

Lady Vesper was staying on at the château until Louisa returned to school and Verian to Oxford. Her husband had been planning a trip to the Chaldees and so her ladyship would spend the winter at the nursing home in Surrey. She urged Hilary to call and see her, but Hilary doubted if Lady Vesper would welcome the sight of her once she had no further need of her services.

So, within a few days, her flight back to London

was arranged and she was confronted with a mere six hours in which to pack and make her adieux.

For a few days Raoul had not been calling at the château; a specialist from Lyons had been coming in his place. When Hilary casually inquired of Lady Vesper why this was so she was told that Raoul was involved with other things and might be giving up the practice.

A thousand questions surged in Hilary's brain, but she knew what she was going to do with two of her six hours, and dressed in a pretty white dress to call on Madame de la Rue. If her son was present so much the better, but she had promised to call once more before her departure for England and intended to honour this.

Madame was lying on a chaise-longue in the old-fashioned garden, at this time of year a riot of geraniums and bougainvillea, and she was touched to see Hilary.

'Come and sit by me, my dear. Raoul has given me no news of you lately, and I wondered if you had gone back home.'

'I fly tonight, from Lyons, to catch the early plane out of Orly, madame.'

'Then we'll have tea and chat a while. I can see you, you know, and how pretty you are! Just as Raoul described you. But you're overworking, my dear. You look tired and—and strained.'

'Things have been a strain just lately,' Hilary admitted.

'Yes, well, you must relax now. Raoul has been looking very tired, too. We have a young man taking over the practice, you know. The authorities have taken over a large mansion, the other side of Aurillac, and invited Raoul to be Director of Paediatrics when they convert it into a children's hospital. Just what he always wanted. I thought he would have been happier than he is about the appointment, but he appears to have taken it in his stride. You and I shall be happy for him, eh, Nurse Hope?'

'Yes. Yes, indeed. Will your son be home soon, madame?'

'He didn't say. I enjoy being independent of him, you know, and he feels freer to stay away than he did before my most fortunate accident.'

They talked on for an hour or more, and Raoul did not come. Hilary felt like weeping as she said goodbye to Madame, and forgot she could see and did allow a tear to spill over.

'I shall tell Raoul you called,' Madame de la Rue said softly, squeezing the girl's hand and wishing she would speak from her heart. She was no fool and understood very well what had started, though she couldn't understand why it had apparently ended like a song in mid-air. 'Would you like to leave a message for him?'

Hilary felt desperate.

'I'll leave my address,' she said, scribbling down the name of the hospital. 'If ever your son is in England he may care to ring me. I must go now. I have to pack.'

Madame reached and kissed her.

'You always do me good,' she said. 'If only Raoul—' she stopped speaking and smiled. 'If mothers picked wives for their sons, I would pick someone exactly like you. *Bon voyage*, my dear. Be happy!'

Raoul came home at a little after ten, astounded at the news that Hilary had visited his mother and already left for the airport. He looked at the slip of paper bearing her address and wanted to know every word she had spoken, even on irrelevant subjects.

'Why did she come now,' he wanted to know, 'when she couldn't be bothered to come after your accident? Maybe there are no young men left at the château,' he added bitterly.

'That's not like you, Raoul,' his mother chided him. 'Hilary is not a butterfly. Something prevented her coming or she would have been my first visitor. I'm sure of that.'

'You have so much faith, Maman, and I so little now. But why should I give her a ring if I go to England? I'm sure there are many English doctors who will dance attendance upon her if that is what she wants.'

Madame sighed, but she noticed he carefully smoothed out the slip of paper Hilary had left and placed it safely away in his pocket-book.

CHAPTER THIRTEEN

THE October day was grey and lowering as Hilary sat down thankfully in the staff dining-room at the hospital for tea. Her feet hurt, and she knew it was because she had been away from the hospital for so long; it would be some time before her body became used once again to the terrific pressures of the life and responded without filling her with twinges in various unexpected places.

Cathy joined her at the table, saying sharply: 'I don't expect I'm welcome. Would you rather do a Garbo and be alone?'

'Of course not, you idiot!' Hilary said quickly. 'Why do you say that?'

'Because you've been a changed person since you came back, honestly, Hope. We all envied you, thinking you were having a whale of a time in *la belle France*, but you haven't been in the least communicative. You act as though you've grown up and still regard the rest of our set as kids. What happened? Am I your chum or not?'

'Of course you're my chum, Cath, but I can't talk about things. Not yet. Do try to understand.'

Cath munched meat paste sandwiches with a youthful appetite.

'O.K., kiddo, I won't pry again after asking one question which is killing me. Maisie Walker reads

The Tatler and knows every eligible young man in society. It appears that the Vespers have a rather beautiful son, about six foot two and blond. Is he all she says, and did you . . . ?'

'Verian *is* all Walker says, and I didn't. If we can all meet together somewhere after duty I'll tell you all about Verian's twenty-first. It was great fun.'

Hiding up a great hollow which had suddenly yawned inside her, she asked: 'How have the bairns been today?'

'Oh, absolute devils. We have a two-and-a-half-year-old miniature Steve McQueen in at present, and the cot hasn't been manufactured which can hold him, or a restrainer. He's emptied the table ink into the biscuit tin, pulled somebody's Teddy's head off to see if he was like little boys inside and used Dr Higgins's stethoscope as a catapult. We'll all merit the George Cross by the time Ian is discharged.'

Cathy sounded happy and tranquil, however, despite these escapades. Her work meant a great deal to her. So far Hilary's did not. She had missed the job on the cardiac ward because Miss Wattkyn did not see why the appointment should be delayed to suit a nurse's convenience. When Hilary explained the situation, which she could now that it was all over to her credit, Matron had been most sympathetic, but explained that she couldn't disappoint Staff Nurse Morris, who was settling down with the cardiacs and doing quite well.

'Of course not, Matron,' Hilary quite agreed. 'I understand perfectly. I suppose I must apply for a job somewhere else.'

Matron considered for a moment.

'Yes, Nurse, I think you should. I could give you a job, and will until you leave us, but you would do very well in a chest hospital, and will soon earn your promotion to Sister in your true *métier*. Perhaps you will transfer to the tutorial side? You have a very good brain. But, in the meantime, Sister Koenig could do with some help in Outpatients.'

So Hilary had been working for ten days in the outpatients' hall, which involved answering numerous questions from people who wanted to know the way to various other departments, attending the specialists during their clinics and doing no actual nursing whatsoever.

So far she had only studied the *Nursing Mirror* desultorily; there were plenty of jobs going for a trained nurse, but she wanted time to think, time to know what she really wanted to do with her life. At the moment she was glad of the hectic existence of Outpatients which tired her body so that her mind refused to function deeply. She felt numb, emotionally, and extremely relieved by the fact.

One day, she knew, she would have to tell Cath about Raoul, but not yet. There was so little to tell, and yet it had been so much that it was, at times, difficult to contemplate life going on without it.

She hadn't heard from Raoul, of course, and didn't really expect to. What he had felt for her was something which he had overcome with apparent ease once he had decided she was not worth the winning.

It was sad, but it was a love that was fated to be lost. Still, it was better to have loved, despite all.

What she had known nobody could take away.

Hearing Cath prattle away about her infants she allowed her attention to wander and jumped when her friend accused: 'You've just agreed that Boris Karloff would make a good nursing Sister. Honestly, Hilary, what *is* wrong with you?'

'Oh, Cath, I'm sorry. I know I'm poor company. Give me time, my dear.'

Cath squeezed her hand and rose.

'I have to get back on duty, not like some people I know who've finished for the night. Are you going out?'

'Yes, I'm going to the pictures,' Hilary decided on impulse. 'I'll call in on you and we'll have cocoa at bedtime if you like.'

A messenger approached as Cath disappeared and told Hilary that Matron would like to see her in her office at once. Wondering what could be amiss, for such a summons usually meant a reprimand for some misdemeanour, Hilary straightened her uniform cap and went down the long corridor to the holy of holies at the double—there were no officious Sisters about to disapprove—and knocked on the door, deciding that if there was to be any unpleasantness it was better to get it over and done with as soon as possible.

Miss Wattkyn sounded quite amiable, however, as she warbled 'Come in!' in her funny contralto voice which was expertly mimicked by the comic in every fresh intake of nurses to the P.T.S.

Hilary entered the room and then gasped as it appeared to spin round and round for a moment or two, for Matron was not alone. From sitting opposite

188

her a man stood up, and a slow smile spread over his countenance as he saw the girl's incredulous stare.

'Hill-ary?' his voice was a question, followed by another one as her eyes dimmed with a sudden flood of tears. 'You are glad to see me?'

She was beside him, both her hands clasped in his as she answered with difficulty, for her lips were trembling and her legs felt weak.

'Oh, Raoul! So very glad. I didn't think—expect—This is such a surprise!'

No one was taking any notice of Matron, so she coughed sharply and reminded her visitors of her existence. 'Very well, Nurse. Dr de la Rue wanted to see you. I should ask for a late pass if I were you, and remember to behave like a nurse until you change out of uniform.'

This was because the said Dr de la Rue had not yet relinquished Hilary's left hand, and as he finally did so, he could not equally discipline his eyes to let the girl slip from their gaze.

Outside the office Hilary did forget she was in uniform while Raoul stooped to kiss her, and for a full five minutes they were lost in forgetfulness, and passers-by duly recorded the scene for the hospital grapevine, which thrived on the happy news that Hilary Hope was very much involved with the most devastatingly handsome man right outside Matron's office, and that it looked like a bad case of happy ever after.

'Good for Hill!' was Cathy's comment, who heard the news when it was half an hour old. 'I knew there was something sadly wrong with her, and as she's had all her injections it *could* only be love. Some people do have all the luck. I wonder if she'll want any bridesmaids.'

In the small restaurant, where they had ordered everything and eaten nothing, Hilary and Raoul had cleared the past of regrets and the future of fears.

'It was Louisa who told me about the burglary,' Raoul explained. 'My mother said it was in the papers later, but I rarely read the papers fully. Louisa fished about you and me; then she said wasn't it a lark that you were suspected and practically kept a prisoner in the house! I said was this so? I thought that was terrible. Why wasn't I told? She said it was her mother's wish that no one should know outside the family and the police kept it dark for obvious reasons. Then I knew—I realised why all happened as it did. Oh, my own sweetheart, I thought you didn't want to—go on with me, marry me and work with me, so very hard. I was too proud to sway you against your will. But all the time . . .'

'All the time I wanted to be swayed, Raoul. I thought you no longer wanted me when you turned so cold.'

'Pride—' Raoul struck his head. 'How poor a substitute is pride for love! But now . . . ?'

She met his eyes with the frankness of her own.

'Now, whatever you wish, Raoul.'

'Then we name the day. I will come back to marry you one month from this day. That will be the seventh of November. You like November for weddings?'

190

'For my wedding, yes, it's perfect,' she laughed delightedly.

'And then we go all over Europe in my car for the honeymoon, nobody but us, together, for one whole month.'

'You still can't scare me off,' she decided.

'After that I find you a job in my hospital. This I promise Mademoiselle Wattkyn when I tell her I want to marry you. Such a waste, she says, of a good nurse if you do not work for a little time.'

'Then I'll work,' Hilary agreed contentedly.

'I think we had better go now,' Raoul decided, drawing her to her feet. 'That man is looking at us strangely. I think he wants to close.'

Outside in the friendly darkness, they walked together, arms entwined, the direction not so important as the fact that they walked together in closeness and harmony; as from now on they would walk through life.

When at last they kissed goodnight under the street lamp at the hospital's main gate, Hilary turned her face up, not only to Raoul, but also to the friendly starlit heavens.

'You were saying something, *chérie*?' he asked her.

'Not really. I was thanking God that I was chosen to perform that holiday task. If it hadn't been for that we would never have met.'

'I would have met you, Hill-ary, if I'd had to swim the Channel to do it. But the main thing is that we did meet, so I will do a little thanking, too.'

He looked up himself into the heavens and regarded the eternal stars for a long, communicative moment, and when he looked down again he wasn't in the least surprised to find that two small stars had been trapped and shone brightly in the eyes of his Hill-ary, his love.